W9-CJB-857

7709

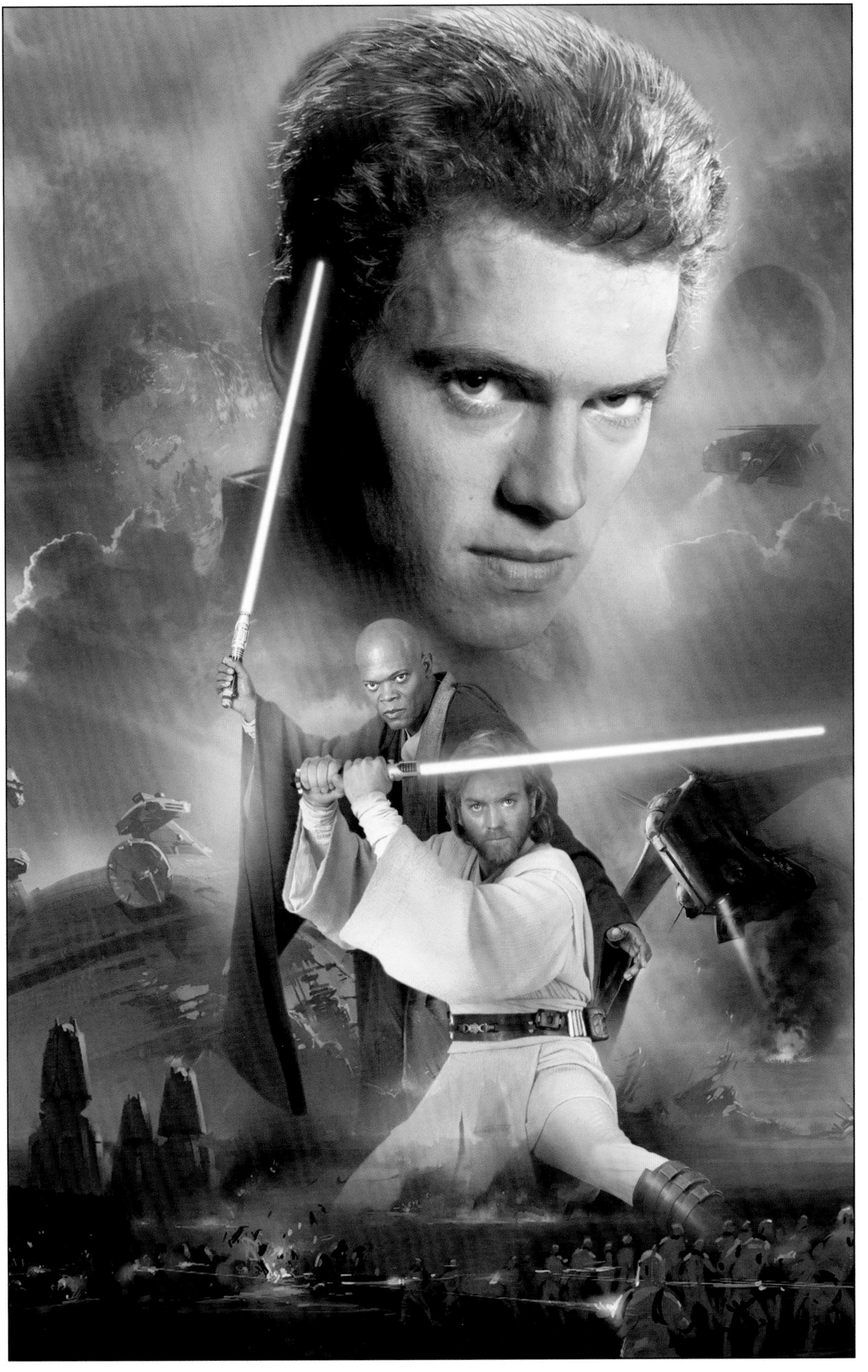

STAR WARS

EPISODE II

ATTACK OF THE CLONES

VOLUME FOUR

ADAPTED BY
HENRY GILROY

BASED ON THE ORIGINAL STORY BY
GEORGE LUCAS

AND THE SCREENPLAY BY
GEORGE LUCAS AND
JONATHAN HALES

PENCILS
JAN DUURSEMA

INKS
RAY KRYSSING

COLORS
**DIGITAL CHAMELEON, DAN JACKSON,
JASON HVAM, DAVID NESTELLE, CHRIS HORN**

COLOR SEPARATOR
HAROLD MACKINNON

LETTERS
STEVE DUTRO

COVER ART
TSUNEO SANDA

DARK
HORSE
COMICS

VISIT US AT
www.abdopublishing.com

Reinforced library bound edition published in 2009 by Spotlight, a division of the ABDO Group, 8000 West 78th Street, Edina, Minnesota 55439. Spotlight produces high-quality reinforced library bound editions for schools and libraries. Published by agreement with Dark Horse Comics, Inc., and Lucasfilm Ltd.

Library of Congress Cataloging-in-Publication Data

Gilroy, Henry.
  Episode II : attack of the clones / story, George Lucas ; script, Henry Gilroy ; pencils, Jan Duursema ; inks, Ray Kryssing ; colors, Dave McCaig ; letters, Steve Dutro. -- Reinforced library bound ed.
     p. cm. -- (Star Wars)
  ISBN 978-1-59961-612-4 (v. 1) -- ISBN 978-1-59961-613-1 (v. 2) – ISBN 978-1-59961-614-8 (v. 3) -- ISBN 978-1-59961-615-5 (v. 4)
  1. Graphic novels. [1. Graphic novels.] I. Lucas, George, 1944- II. Duursema, Jan, ill. III. Kryssing, Ray. IV. McCaig, Dave. V. Dutro, Steve. VI. Star wars, episode II, attack of the clones (Motion picture) VII. Title.
  PZ7.7.G55Epl 2009
  [Fic]--dc22
                              2008038311

All Spotlight books have reinforced library bindings and are manufactured in the United States of America.

Episode II

ATTACK OF THE CLONES

Volume 4

Jedi Obi-Wan Kenobi has pursued the bounty hunter Jango Fett to Geonosis, where Count Dooku—leader of the Separatists—reveals his droid army and signs a treaty to join with the Corporate Alliance and the Commerce Guild against the Republic.

While transmitting a message to the Jedi Council and his Padawan Anakin Skywalker, Obi-Wan is discovered and captured.

Anakin and Senator Amidala defy Obi-Wan's orders to remain safe. They leave immediately with hopes of saving their friend, but both are captured shortly after their arrival on Geonosis . . .

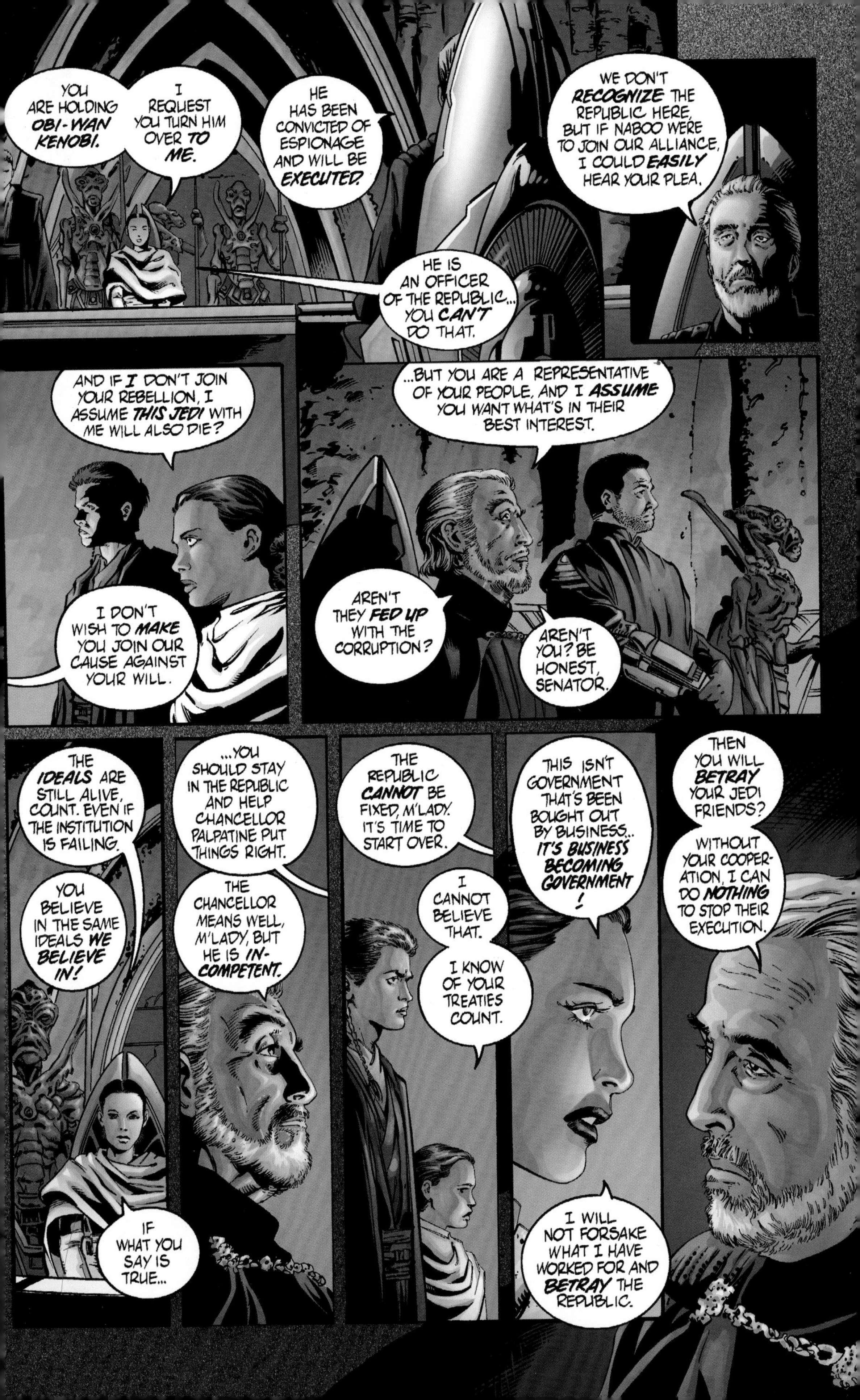
YOU ARE HOLDING OBI-WAN KENOBI.
I REQUEST YOU TURN HIM OVER TO ME.
HE HAS BEEN CONVICTED OF ESPIONAGE AND WILL BE EXECUTED.
HE IS AN OFFICER OF THE REPUBLIC... YOU CAN'T DO THAT.
WE DON'T RECOGNIZE THE REPUBLIC HERE, BUT IF NABOO WERE TO JOIN OUR ALLIANCE, I COULD EASILY HEAR YOUR PLEA.
AND IF I DON'T JOIN YOUR REBELLION, I ASSUME THIS JEDI WITH ME WILL ALSO DIE?
I DON'T WISH TO MAKE YOU JOIN OUR CAUSE AGAINST YOUR WILL.
...BUT YOU ARE A REPRESENTATIVE OF YOUR PEOPLE, AND I ASSUME YOU WANT WHAT'S IN THEIR BEST INTEREST.
AREN'T THEY FED UP WITH THE CORRUPTION?
AREN'T YOU? BE HONEST, SENATOR.
THE IDEALS ARE STILL ALIVE, COUNT. EVEN IF THE INSTITUTION IS FAILING.
YOU BELIEVE IN THE SAME IDEALS WE BELIEVE IN!
IF WHAT YOU SAY IS TRUE...
...YOU SHOULD STAY IN THE REPUBLIC AND HELP CHANCELLOR PALPATINE PUT THINGS RIGHT.
THE CHANCELLOR MEANS WELL, M'LADY, BUT HE IS IN-COMPETENT.
THE REPUBLIC CANNOT BE FIXED, M'LADY. IT'S TIME TO START OVER.
I CANNOT BELIEVE THAT.
I KNOW OF YOUR TREATIES COUNT.
THIS ISN'T GOVERNMENT THAT'S BEEN BOUGHT OUT BY BUSINESS... IT'S BUSINESS BECOMING GOVERNMENT!
I WILL NOT FORSAKE WHAT I HAVE WORKED FOR AND BETRAY THE REPUBLIC.
THEN YOU WILL BETRAY YOUR JEDI FRIENDS?
WITHOUT YOUR COOPER-ATION, I CAN DO NOTHING TO STOP THEIR EXECUTION.

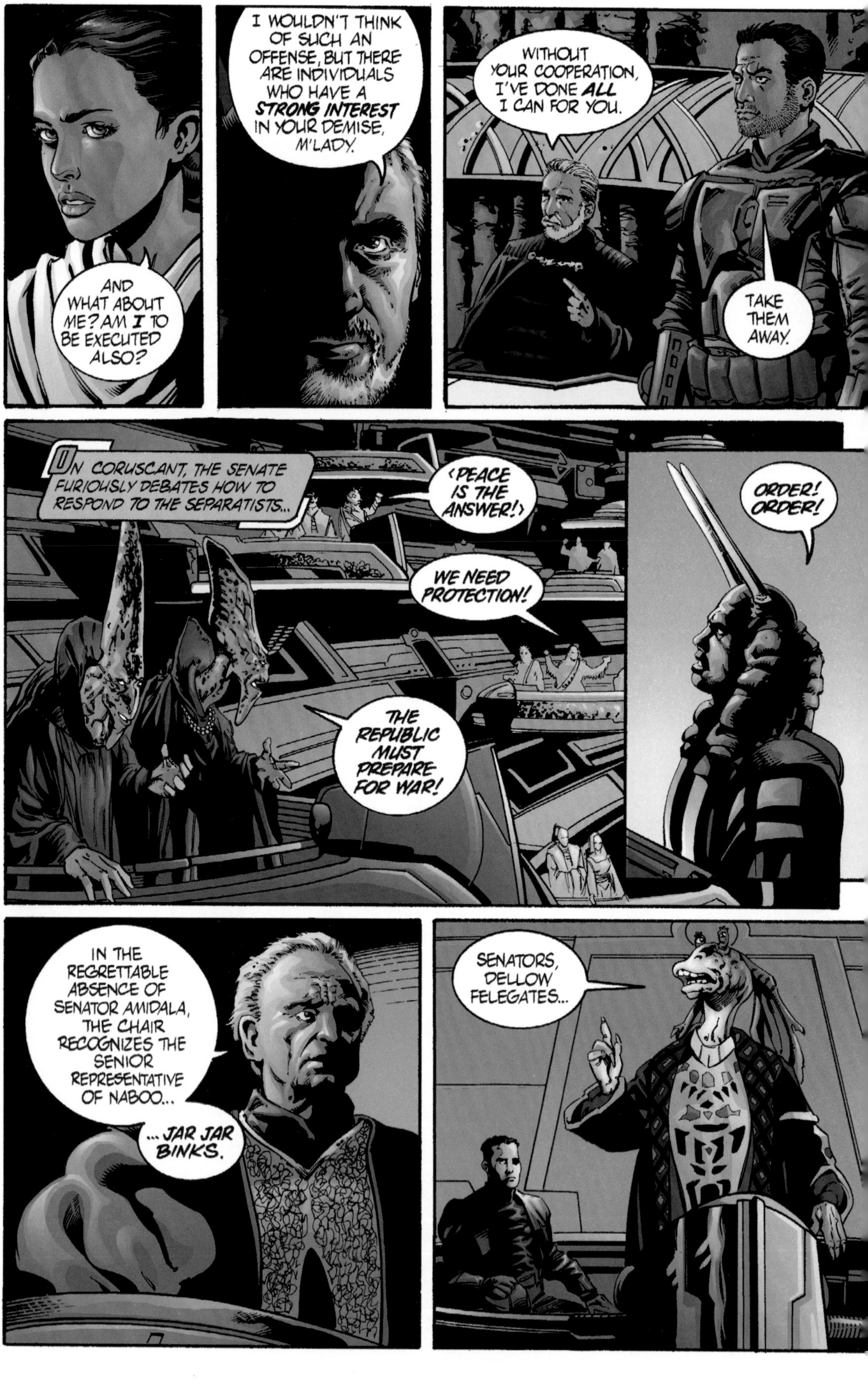
AND WHAT ABOUT ME? AM I TO BE EXECUTED ALSO?
I WOULDN'T THINK OF SUCH AN OFFENSE, BUT THERE ARE INDIVIDUALS WHO HAVE A STRONG INTEREST IN YOUR DEMISE, M'LADY.
WITHOUT YOUR COOPERATION, I'VE DONE ALL I CAN FOR YOU.
TAKE THEM AWAY.
ON CORUSCANT, THE SENATE FURIOUSLY DEBATES HOW TO RESPOND TO THE SEPARATISTS...
‹PEACE IS THE ANSWER!›
WE NEED PROTECTION!
THE REPUBLIC MUST PREPARE FOR WAR!
ORDER! ORDER!
IN THE REGRETTABLE ABSENCE OF SENATOR AMIDALA, THE CHAIR RECOGNIZES THE SENIOR REPRESENTATIVE OF NABOO...
...JAR JAR BINKS.
SENATORS, DELLOW FELEGATES...

IN RESPONSE TO THE DIRECT THREAT TO THE REPUBLIC, *MEESA* PROPOSE THAT THE SENATE GIVE IMMEDIATELY EMERGENCY POWERS TO...

...THE SUPREME CHANCELLOR!

JAR JAR'S SURPRISING PROPOSITION IS MET WITH WILD APPROVAL BY THE SENATE...

AT LAST! WE'RE SAVED!

...MUCH TO THE GUNGAN DIPLOMAT'S DELIGHT.

IT IS WITH GREAT RELUCTANCE THAT I HAVE AGREED TO THIS CALLING. I LOVE DEMOCRACY... I LOVE THE REPUBLIC.

BUT I AM MILD BY NATURE, AND I DO NOT DESIRE TO SEE THE *DESTRUCTION* OF DEMOCRACY.

THE POWER YOU GIVE ME I WILL LAY DOWN WHEN THIS CRISIS HAS ABATED, *I PROMISE YOU.*

AND AS MY FIRST ACT WITH THIS NEW AUTHORITY...

...I WILL CREATE A GRAND ARMY OF THE REPUBLIC TO COUNTER THE INCREASING THREATS OF THE SEPARATISTS.

IT IS DONE, THEN.

I WILL TAKE THE JEDI WE HAVE LEFT AND GO TO GEONOSIS AND HELP OBI-WAN.

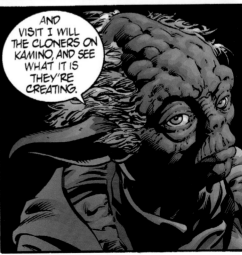

AND VISIT I WILL THE CLONERS ON KAMINO, AND SEE WHAT IT IS THEY'RE CREATING.

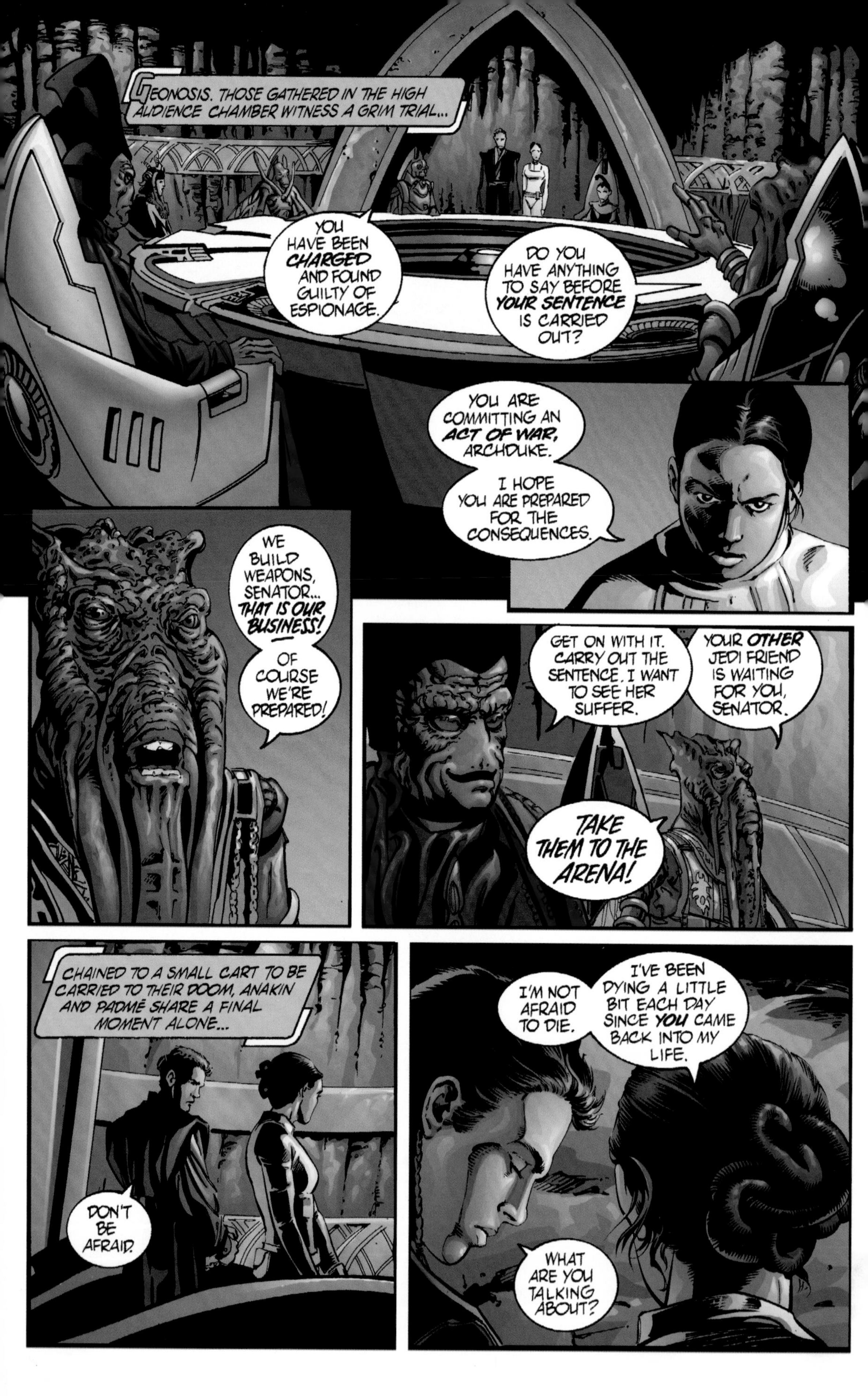
GEONOSIS. THOSE GATHERED IN THE HIGH AUDIENCE CHAMBER WITNESS A GRIM TRIAL...
YOU HAVE BEEN CHARGED AND FOUND GUILTY OF ESPIONAGE.
DO YOU HAVE ANYTHING TO SAY BEFORE YOUR SENTENCE IS CARRIED OUT?
YOU ARE COMMITTING AN ACT OF WAR, ARCHDUKE.
I HOPE YOU ARE PREPARED FOR THE CONSEQUENCES.
WE BUILD WEAPONS, SENATOR... THAT IS OUR BUSINESS!
OF COURSE WE'RE PREPARED!
GET ON WITH IT. CARRY OUT THE SENTENCE. I WANT TO SEE HER SUFFER.
YOUR OTHER JEDI FRIEND IS WAITING FOR YOU, SENATOR.
TAKE THEM TO THE ARENA!
CHAINED TO A SMALL CART TO BE CARRIED TO THEIR DOOM, ANAKIN AND PADMÉ SHARE A FINAL MOMENT ALONE...
DON'T BE AFRAID.
I'M NOT AFRAID TO DIE.
I'VE BEEN DYING A LITTLE BIT EACH DAY SINCE YOU CAME BACK INTO MY LIFE.
WHAT ARE YOU TALKING ABOUT?

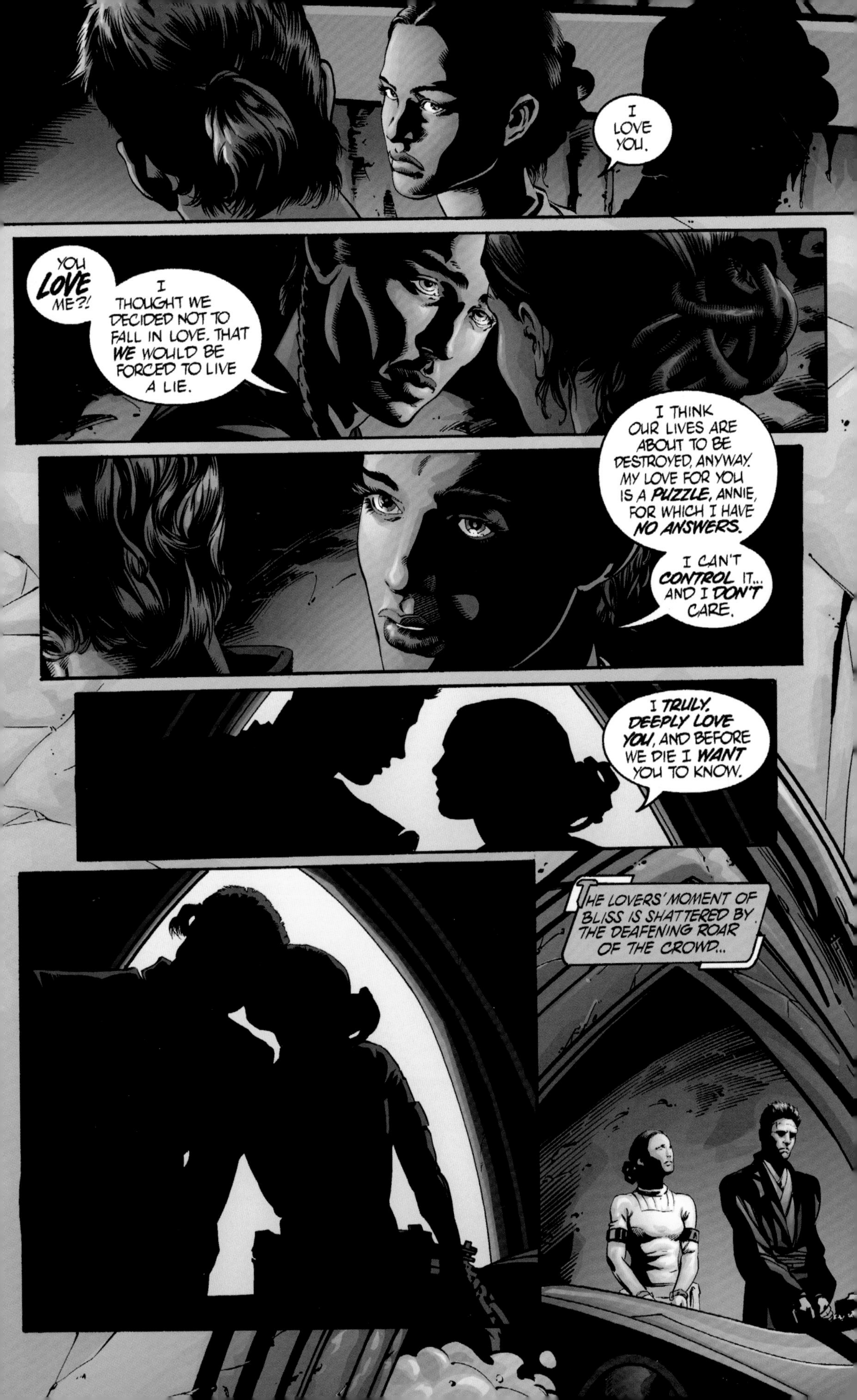
I LOVE YOU.
YOU LOVE ME?!
I THOUGHT WE DECIDED NOT TO FALL IN LOVE. THAT WE WOULD BE FORCED TO LIVE A LIE.
I THINK OUR LIVES ARE ABOUT TO BE DESTROYED, ANYWAY. MY LOVE FOR YOU IS A PUZZLE, ANNIE, FOR WHICH I HAVE NO ANSWERS.
I CAN'T CONTROL IT... AND I DON'T CARE.
I TRULY, DEEPLY LOVE YOU, AND BEFORE WE DIE I WANT YOU TO KNOW.
THE LOVERS' MOMENT OF BLISS IS SHATTERED BY THE DEAFENING ROAR OF THE CROWD...

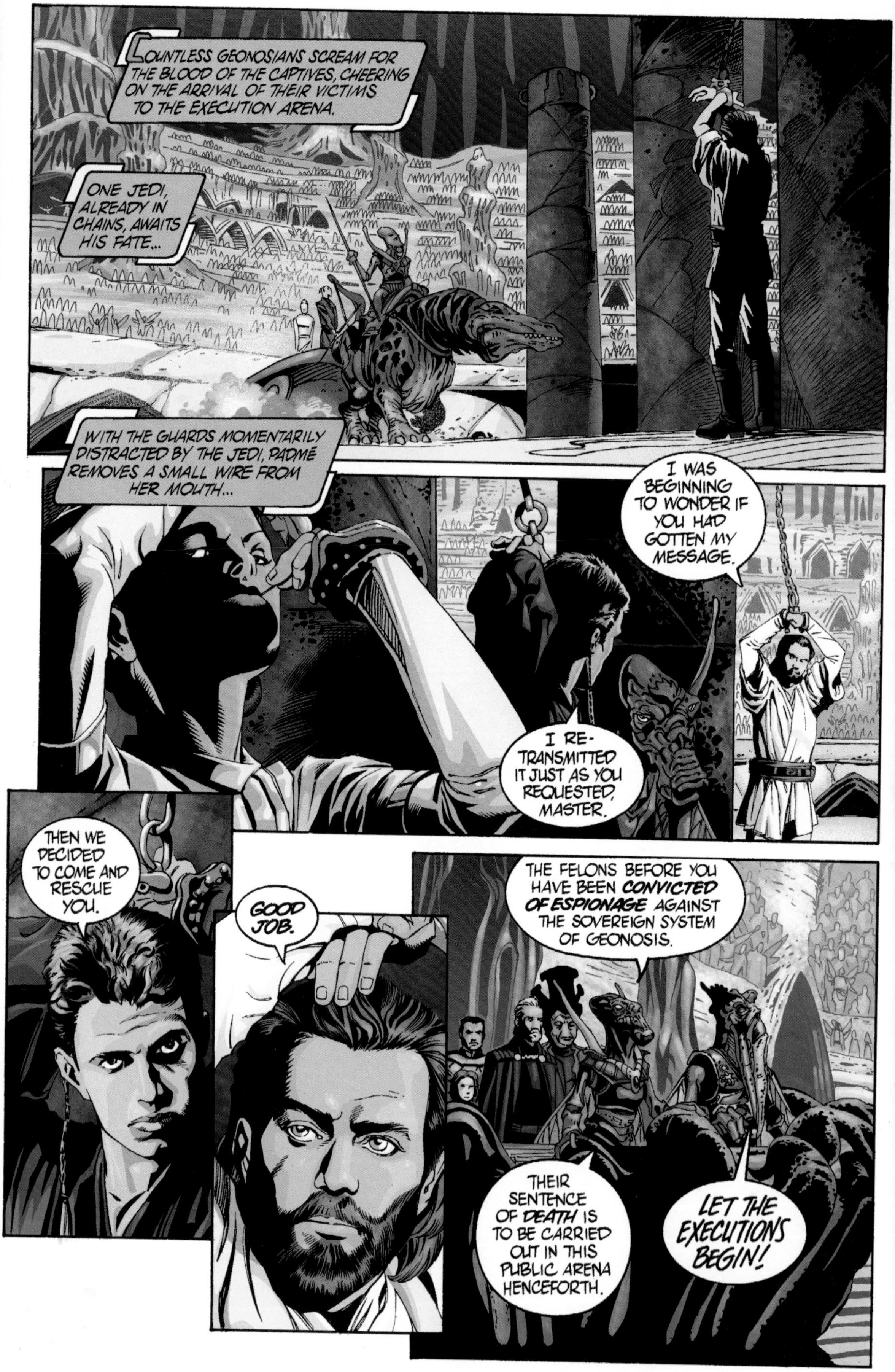
COUNTLESS GEONOSIANS SCREAM FOR THE BLOOD OF THE CAPTIVES, CHEERING ON THE ARRIVAL OF THEIR VICTIMS TO THE EXECUTION ARENA.
ONE JEDI, ALREADY IN CHAINS, AWAITS HIS FATE...
WITH THE GUARDS MOMENTARILY DISTRACTED BY THE JEDI, PADMÉ REMOVES A SMALL WIRE FROM HER MOUTH...
I WAS BEGINNING TO WONDER IF YOU HAD GOTTEN MY MESSAGE.
I RE-TRANSMITTED IT JUST AS YOU REQUESTED, MASTER.
THEN WE DECIDED TO COME AND RESCUE YOU.
GOOD JOB.
THE FELONS BEFORE YOU HAVE BEEN CONVICTED OF ESPIONAGE AGAINST THE SOVEREIGN SYSTEM OF GEONOSIS.
THEIR SENTENCE OF DEATH IS TO BE CARRIED OUT IN THIS PUBLIC ARENA HENCEFORTH.
LET THE EXECUTIONS BEGIN!

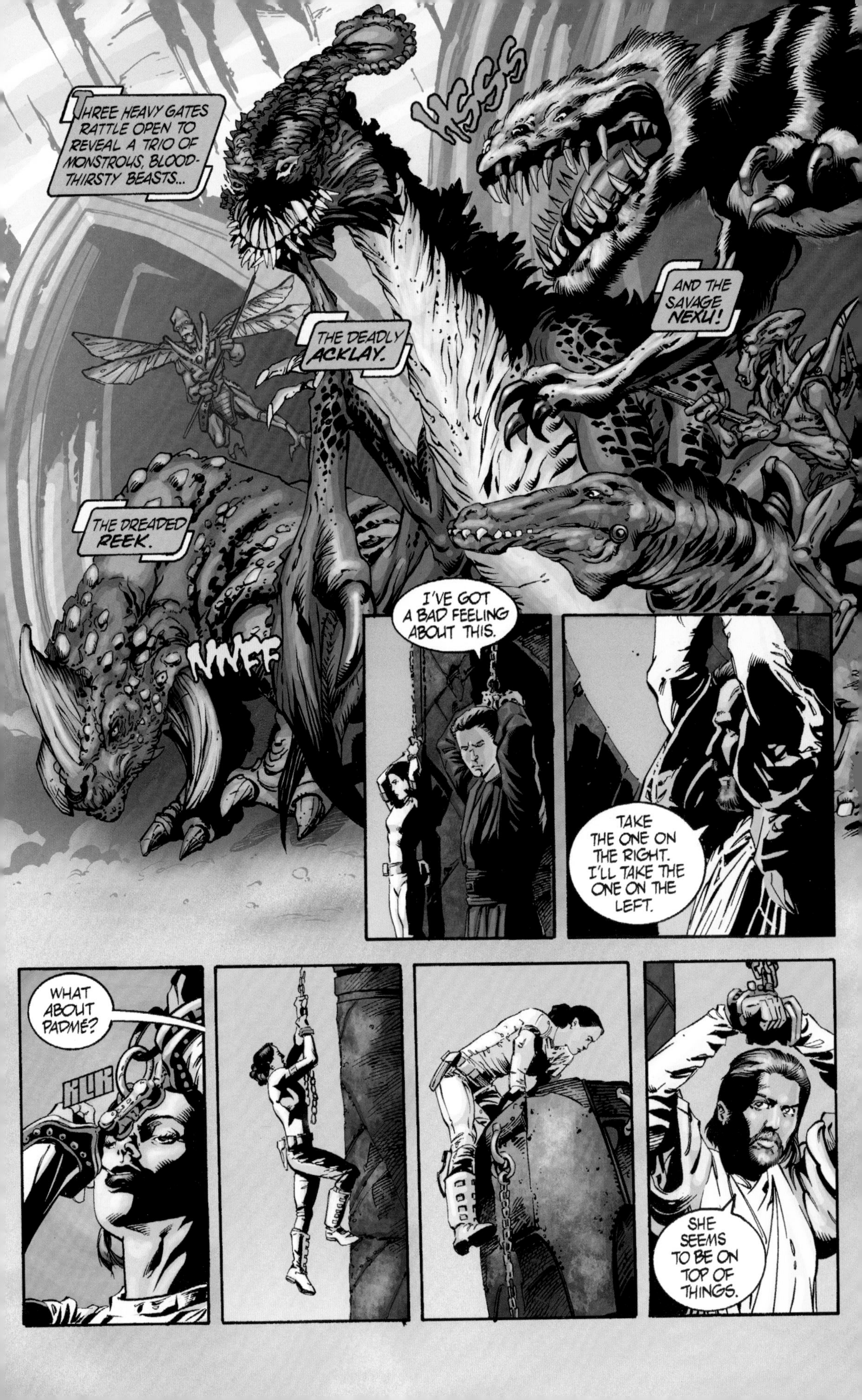

THREE HEAVY GATES RATTLE OPEN TO REVEAL A TRIO OF MONSTROUS, BLOOD-THIRSTY BEASTS...
KSSS
THE DEADLY ACKLAY.
AND THE SAVAGE NEXU!
THE DREADED REEK.
NNFF
I'VE GOT A BAD FEELING ABOUT THIS.
TAKE THE ONE ON THE RIGHT. I'LL TAKE THE ONE ON THE LEFT.
WHAT ABOUT PADMÉ?
KLIK
SHE SEEMS TO BE ON TOP OF THINGS.

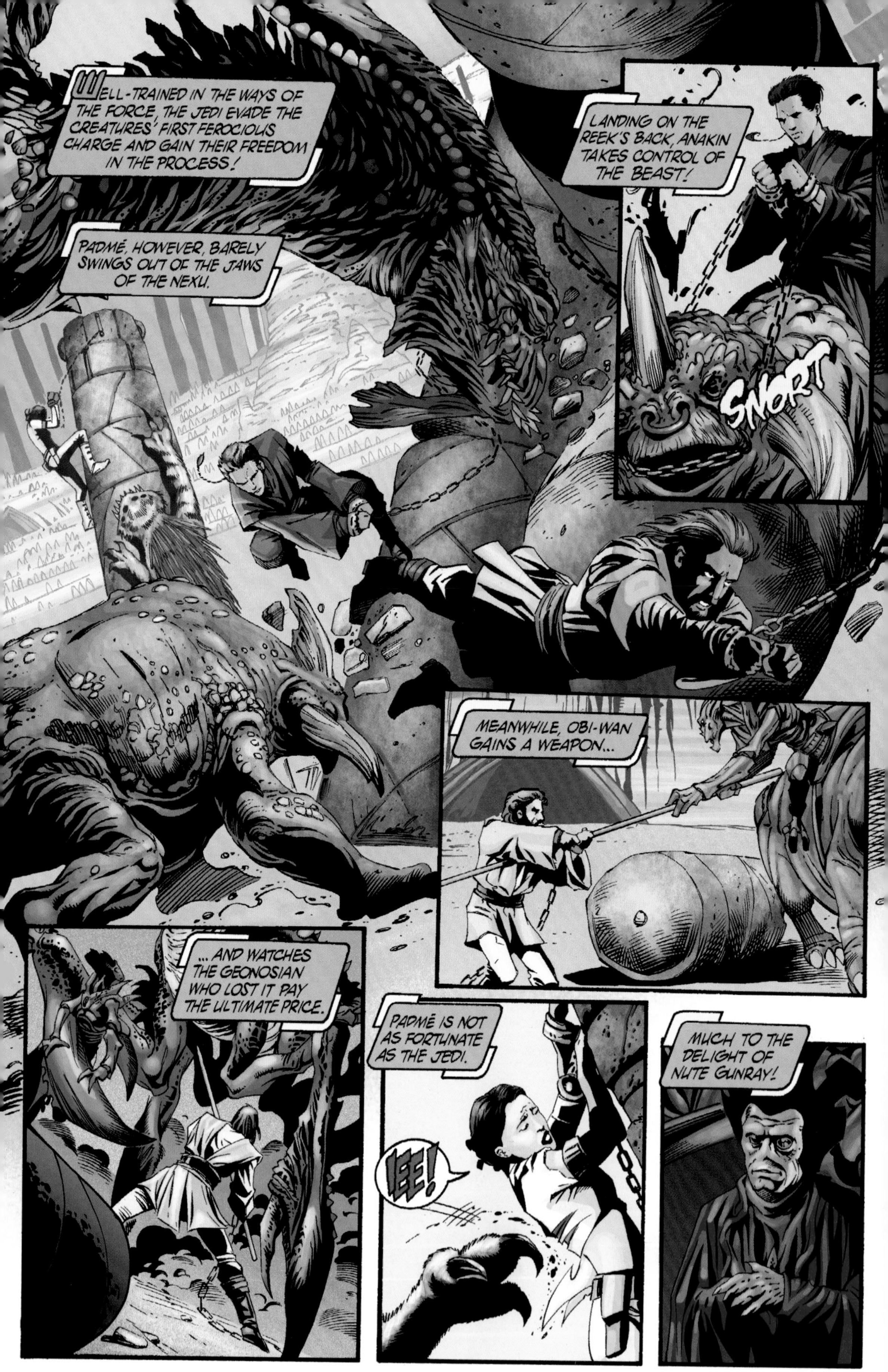
WELL-TRAINED IN THE WAYS OF THE FORCE, THE JEDI EVADE THE CREATURES' FIRST FEROCIOUS CHARGE AND GAIN THEIR FREEDOM IN THE PROCESS!
LANDING ON THE REEK'S BACK, ANAKIN TAKES CONTROL OF THE BEAST!
SNORT
PADMÉ, HOWEVER, BARELY SWINGS OUT OF THE JAWS OF THE NEXU.
MEANWHILE, OBI-WAN GAINS A WEAPON...
...AND WATCHES THE GEONOSIAN WHO LOST IT PAY THE ULTIMATE PRICE.
PADMÉ IS NOT AS FORTUNATE AS THE JEDI.
IEE!
MUCH TO THE DELIGHT OF NUTE GUNRAY!

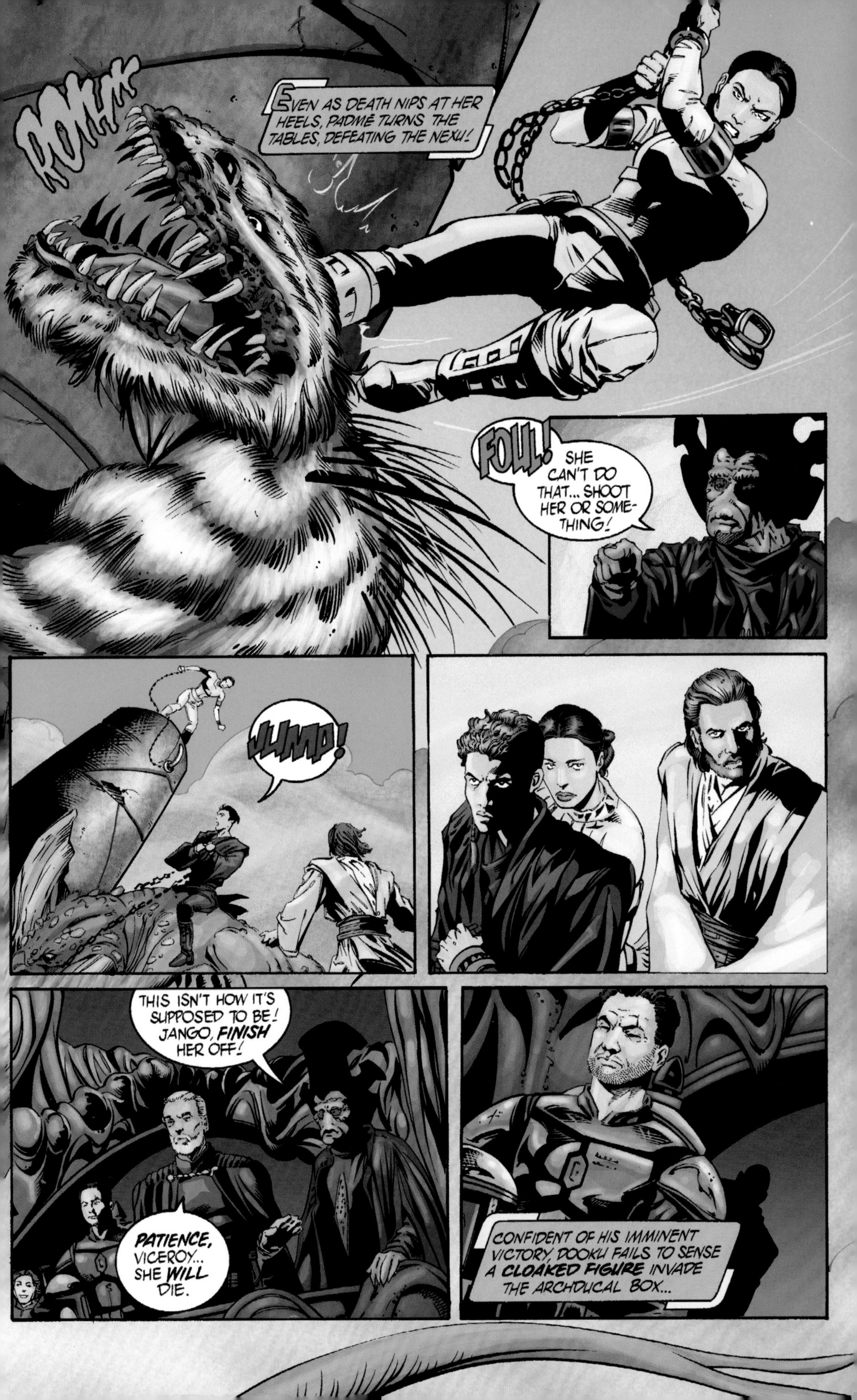
ROWR
EVEN AS DEATH NIPS AT HER HEELS, PADMÉ TURNS THE TABLES, DEFEATING THE NEXU!
FOUL!
SHE CAN'T DO THAT... SHOOT HER OR SOME-THING!
JUMP!
THIS ISN'T HOW IT'S SUPPOSED TO BE! JANGO, FINISH HER OFF!
PATIENCE, VICEROY... SHE WILL DIE.
CONFIDENT OF HIS IMMINENT VICTORY, DOOKU FAILS TO SENSE A CLOAKED FIGURE INVADE THE ARCHDUCAL BOX...

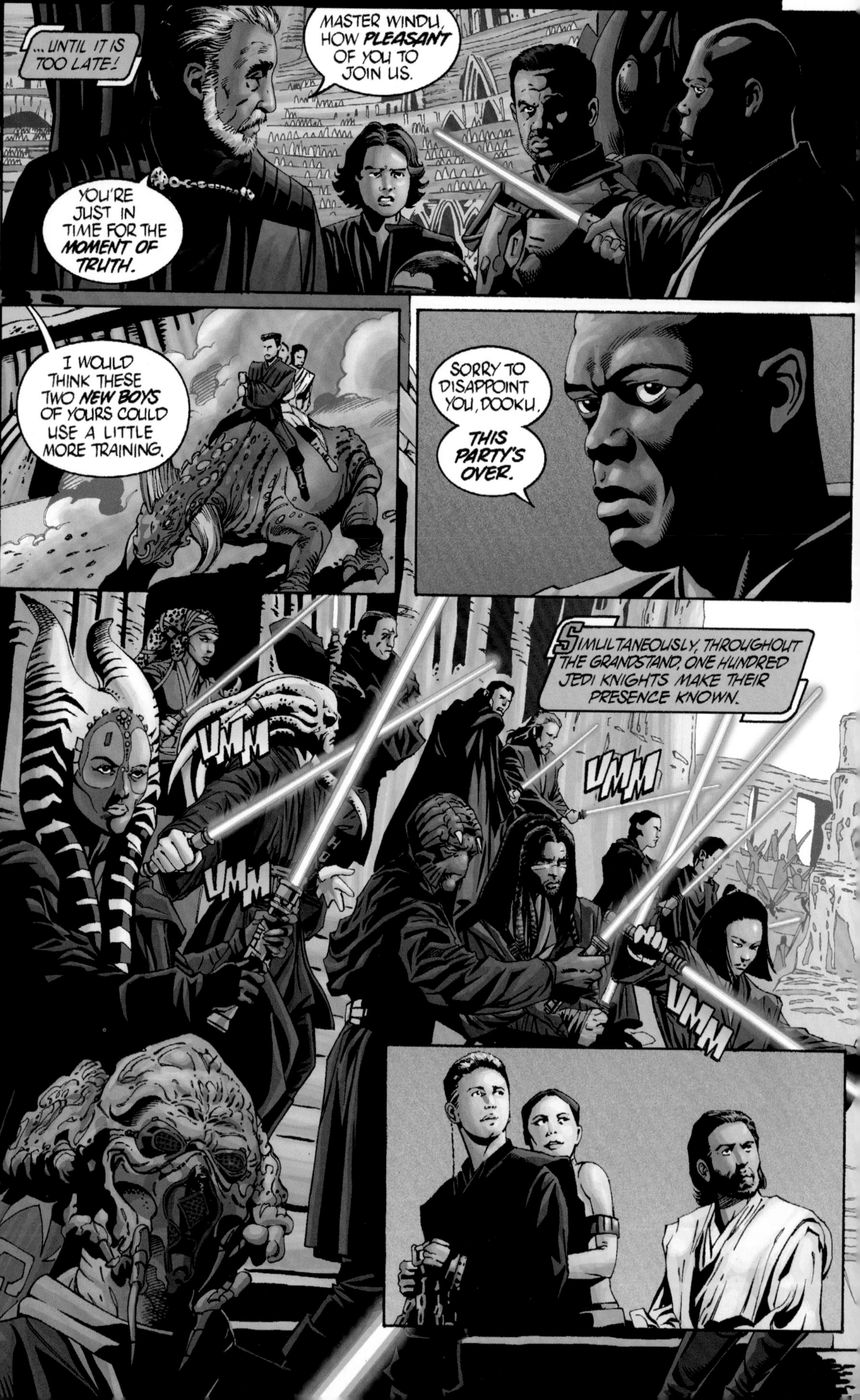

...UNTIL IT IS TOO LATE!
MASTER WINDU, HOW PLEASANT OF YOU TO JOIN US.
YOU'RE JUST IN TIME FOR THE MOMENT OF TRUTH.
I WOULD THINK THESE TWO NEW BOYS OF YOURS COULD USE A LITTLE MORE TRAINING.
SORRY TO DISAPPOINT YOU, DOOKU.
THIS PARTY'S OVER.
SIMULTANEOUSLY, THROUGHOUT THE GRANDSTAND, ONE HUNDRED JEDI KNIGHTS MAKE THEIR PRESENCE KNOWN.
UMM
UMM
UMM
UMM

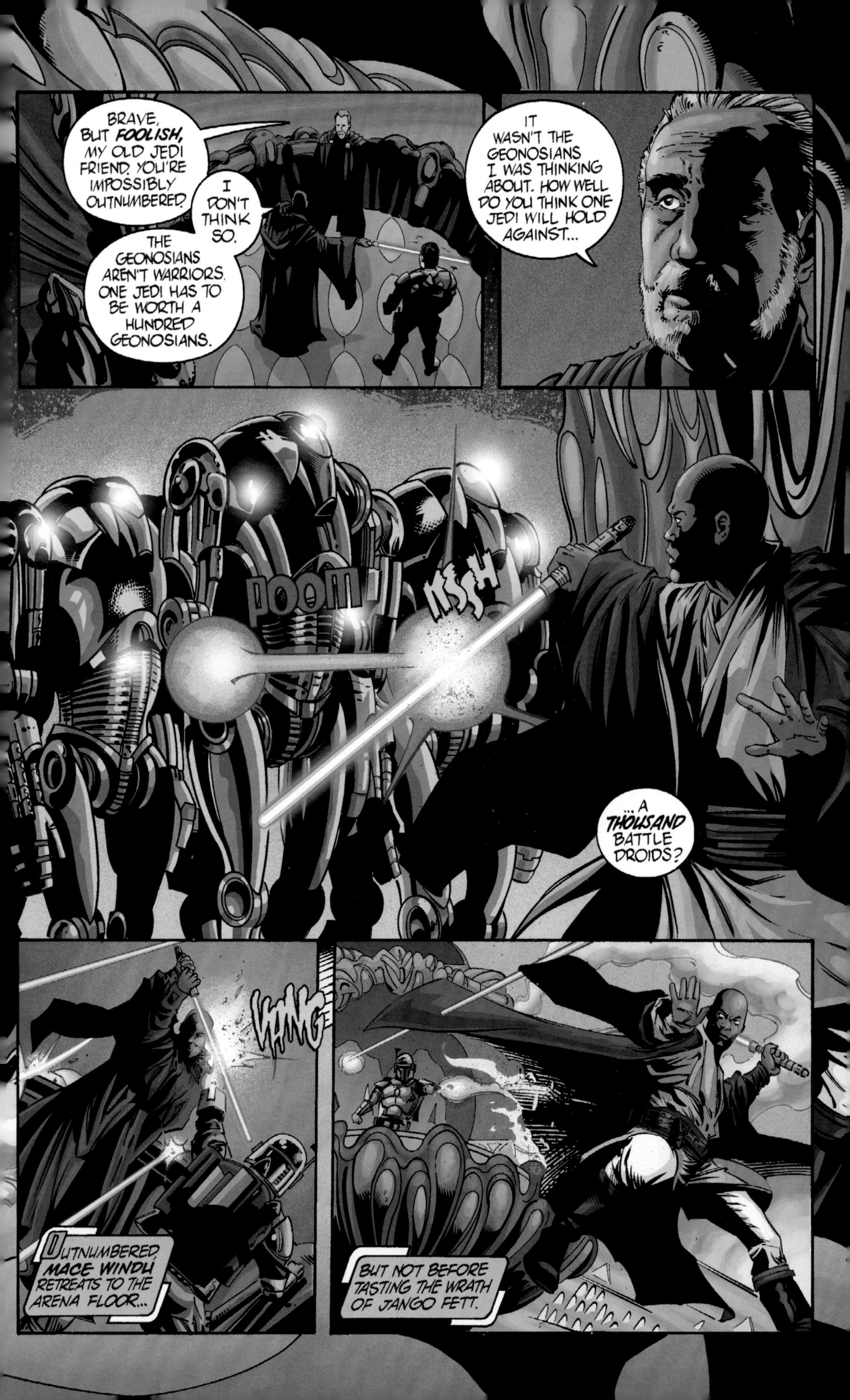
BRAVE, BUT FOOLISH, MY OLD JEDI FRIEND. YOU'RE IMPOSSIBLY OUTNUMBERED.
I DON'T THINK SO.
THE GEONOSIANS AREN'T WARRIORS. ONE JEDI HAS TO BE WORTH A HUNDRED GEONOSIANS.
IT WASN'T THE GEONOSIANS I WAS THINKING ABOUT. HOW WELL DO YOU THINK ONE JEDI WILL HOLD AGAINST...
POOM
KSSH
...A THOUSAND BATTLE DROIDS?
VANG
OUTNUMBERED MACE WINDU RETREATS TO THE ARENA FLOOR...
BUT NOT BEFORE TASTING THE WRATH OF JANGO FETT.

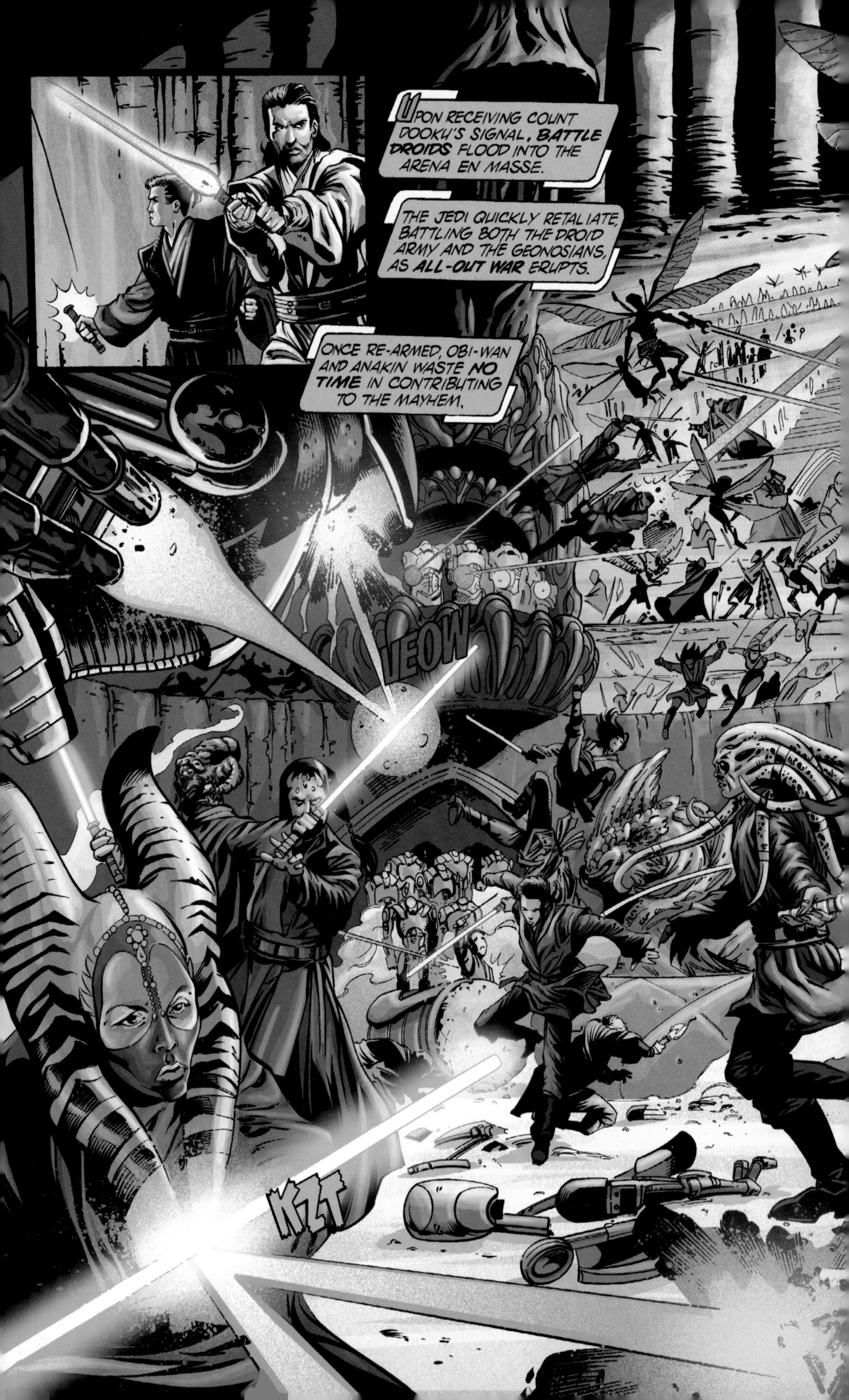
UPON RECEIVING COUNT DOOKU'S SIGNAL, BATTLE DROIDS FLOOD INTO THE ARENA EN MASSE.
THE JEDI QUICKLY RETALIATE, BATTLING BOTH THE DROID ARMY AND THE GEONOSIANS, AS ALL-OUT WAR ERUPTS.
ONCE RE-ARMED, OBI-WAN AND ANAKIN WASTE NO TIME IN CONTRIBUTING TO THE MAYHEM.
VEOW
KZZT

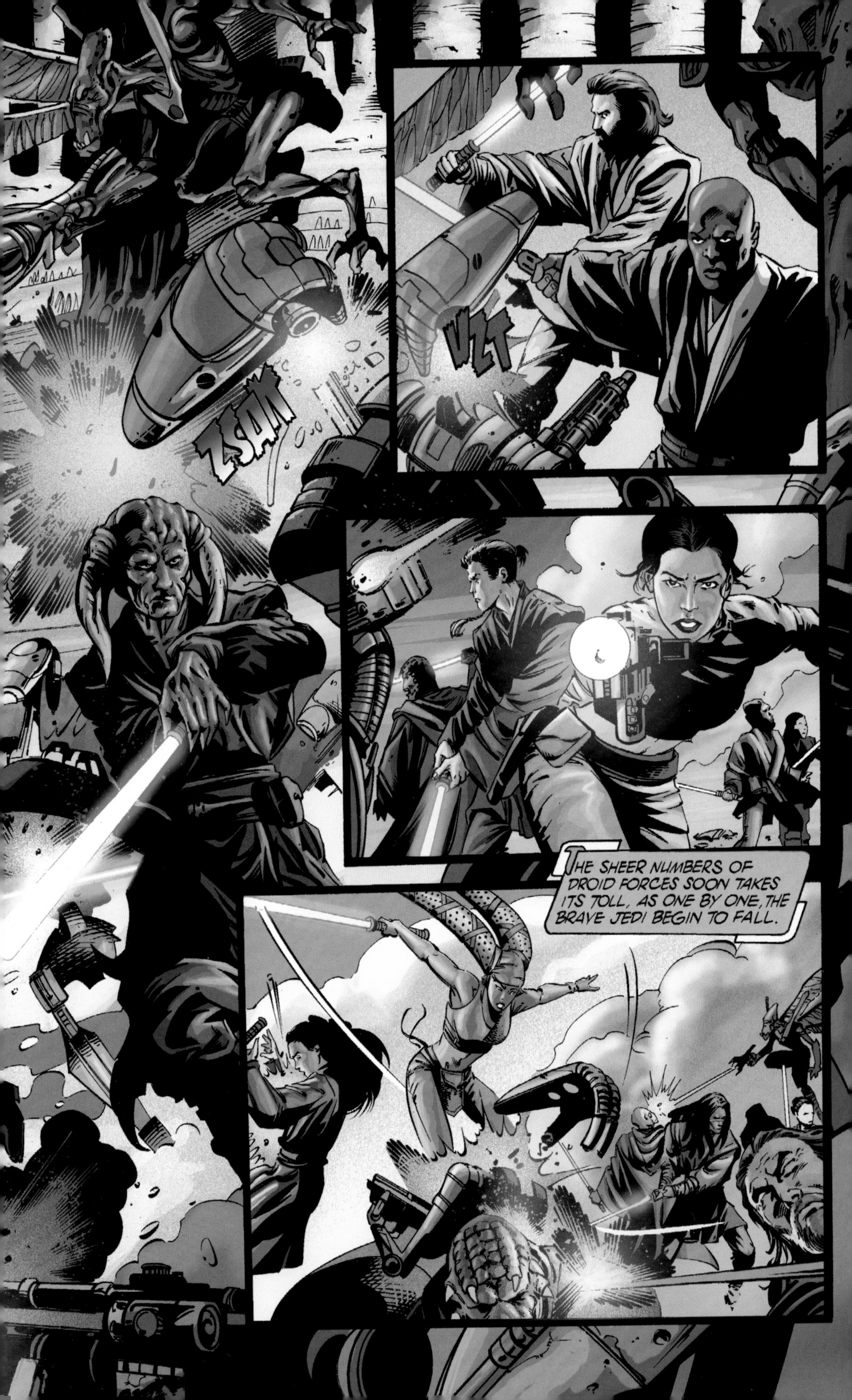
ZSAK
VZT
THE SHEER NUMBERS OF DROID FORCES SOON TAKES ITS TOLL, AS ONE BY ONE, THE BRAVE JEDI BEGIN TO FALL.

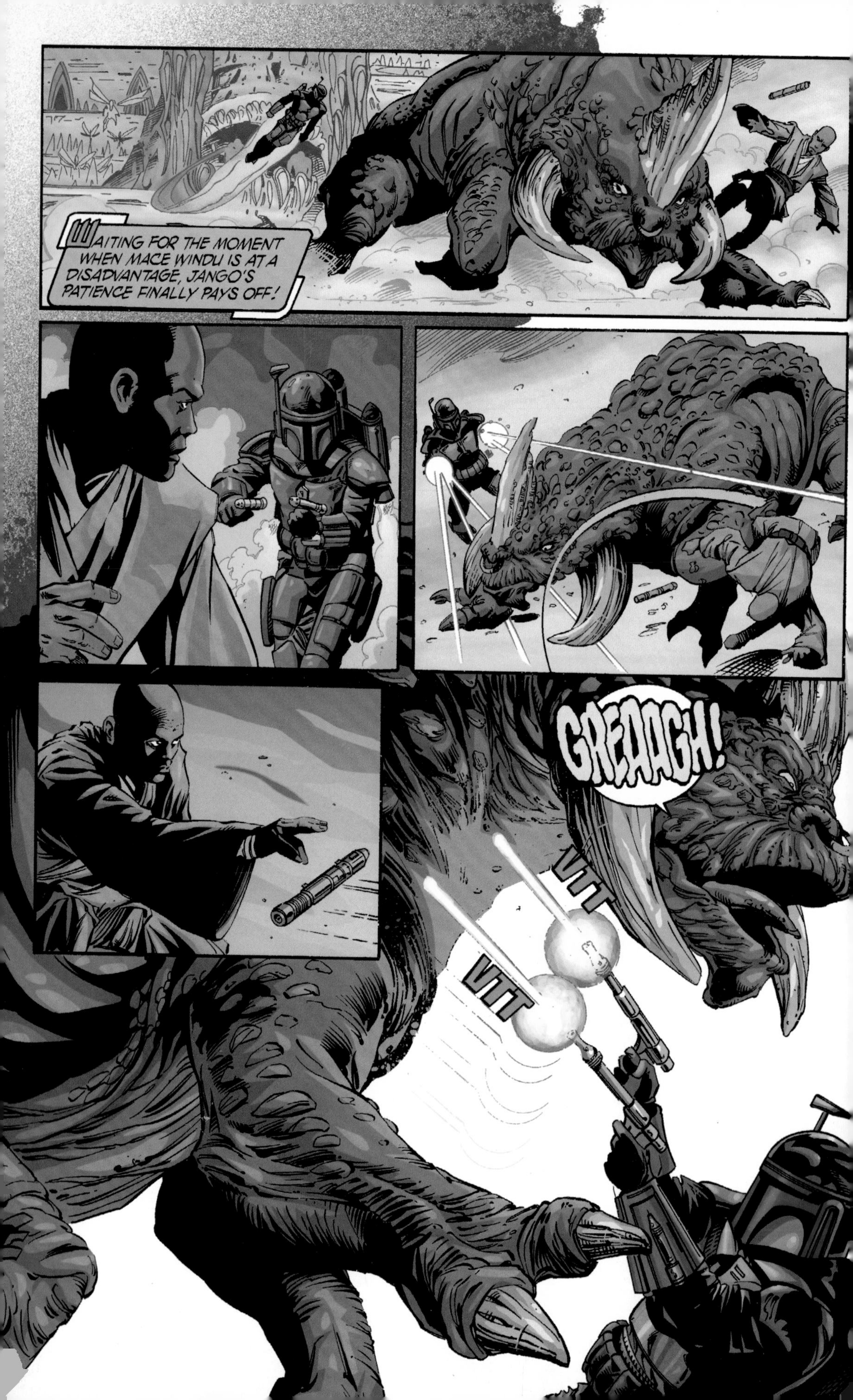
WAITING FOR THE MOMENT WHEN MACE WINDU IS AT A DISADVANTAGE, JANGO'S PATIENCE FINALLY PAYS OFF!
GREAAGH!
VIT
VIT

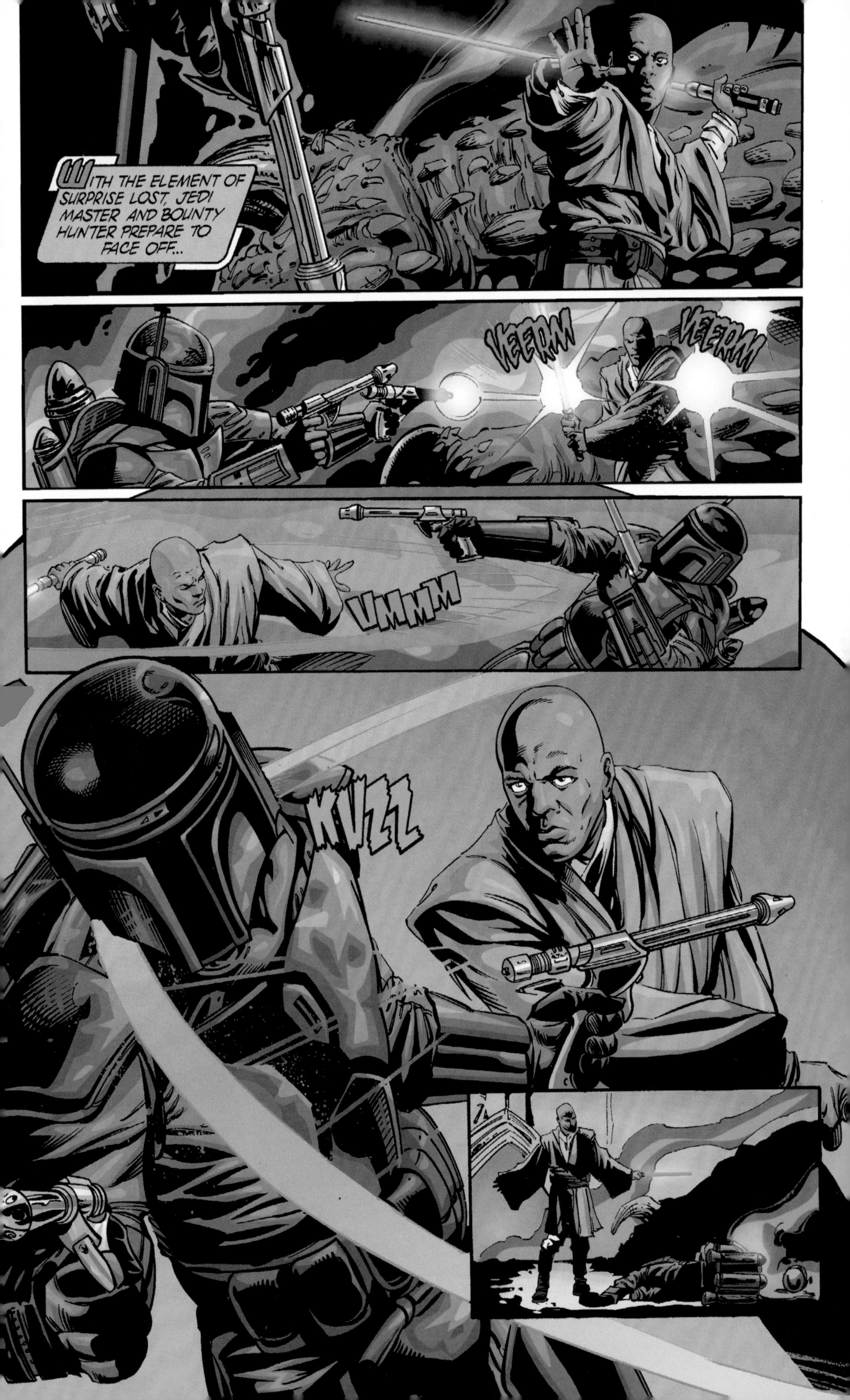
WITH THE ELEMENT OF SURPRISE LOST, JEDI MASTER AND BOUNTY HUNTER PREPARE TO FACE OFF...
VEERM
VEERM
UMMM
KVZZ

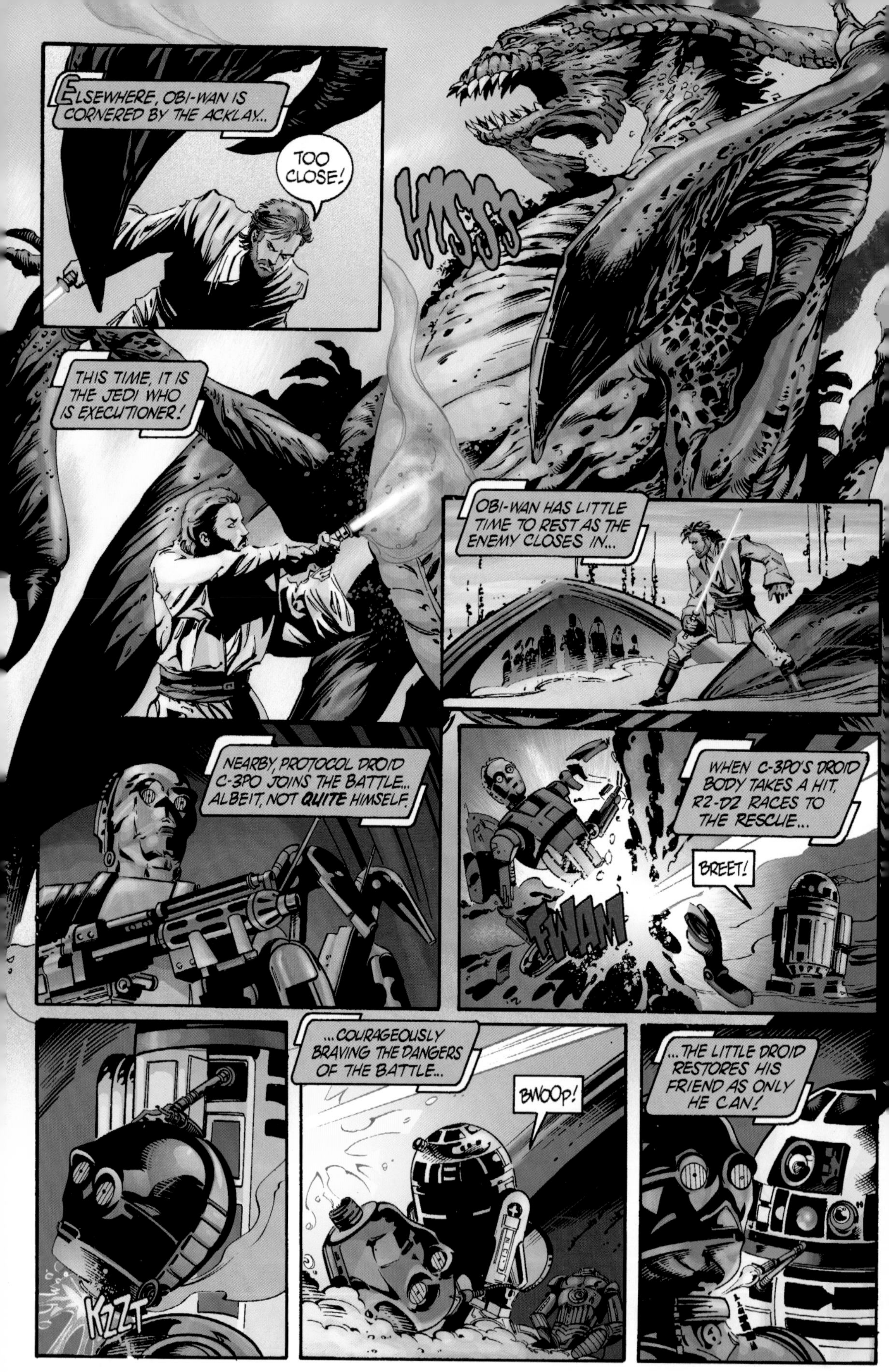
ELSEWHERE, OBI-WAN IS CORNERED BY THE ACKLAY...
TOO CLOSE!
HISSSS
THIS TIME, IT IS THE JEDI WHO IS EXECUTIONER!
OBI-WAN HAS LITTLE TIME TO REST AS THE ENEMY CLOSES IN...
NEARBY, PROTOCOL DROID C-3PO JOINS THE BATTLE... ALBEIT, NOT QUITE HIMSELF.
WHEN C-3PO'S DROID BODY TAKES A HIT, R2-D2 RACES TO THE RESCUE...
BREET!
FWAM
KZZT
...COURAGEOUSLY BRAVING THE DANGERS OF THE BATTLE...
BWOOP!
...THE LITTLE DROID RESTORES HIS FRIEND AS ONLY HE CAN!

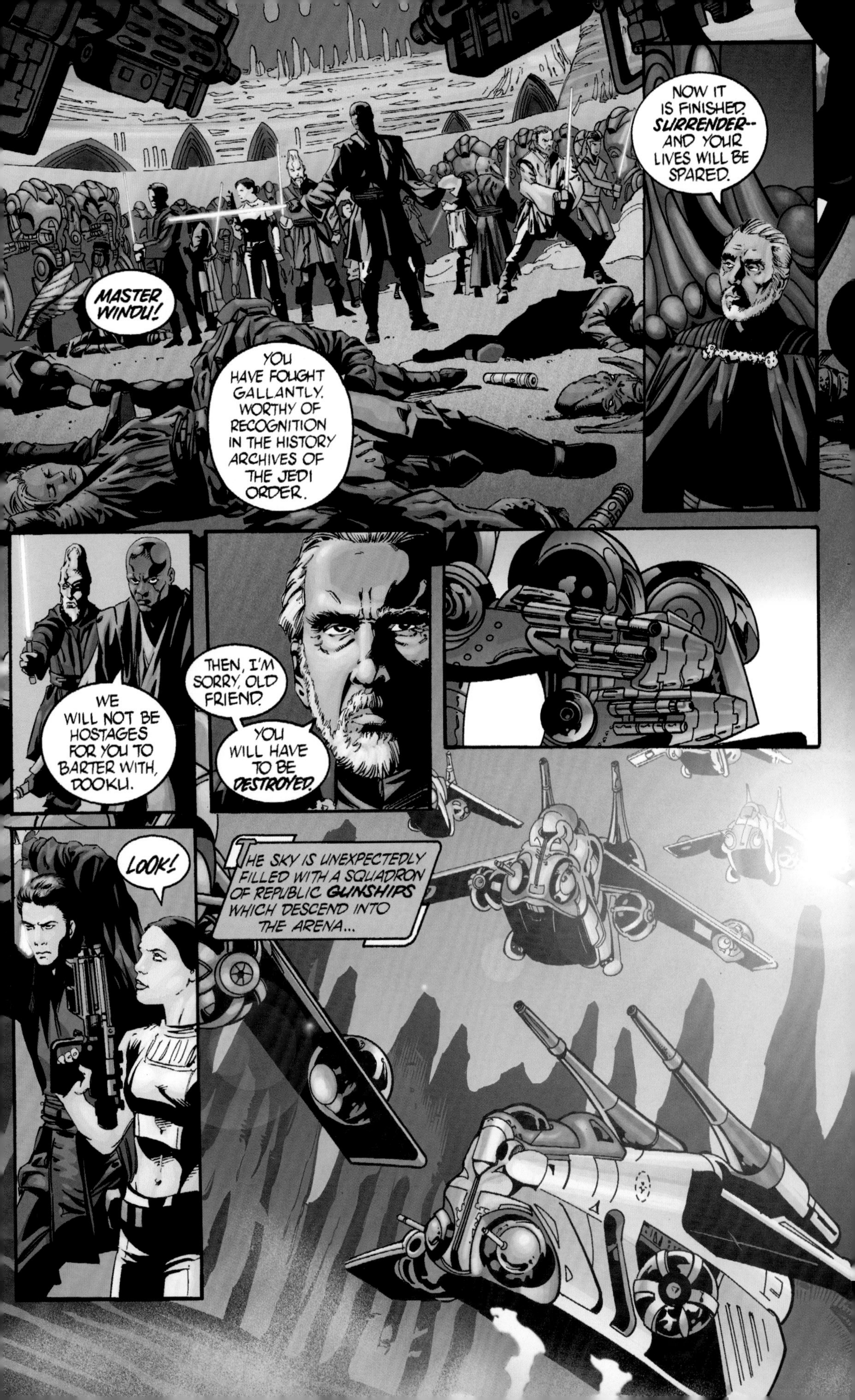
NOW IT IS FINISHED. SURRENDER-- AND YOUR LIVES WILL BE SPARED.
MASTER WINDU!
YOU HAVE FOUGHT GALLANTLY. WORTHY OF RECOGNITION IN THE HISTORY ARCHIVES OF THE JEDI ORDER.
WE WILL NOT BE HOSTAGES FOR YOU TO BARTER WITH, DOOKU.
THEN, I'M SORRY, OLD FRIEND.
YOU WILL HAVE TO BE DESTROYED.
LOOK!
THE SKY IS UNEXPECTEDLY FILLED WITH A SQUADRON OF REPUBLIC GUNSHIPS WHICH DESCEND INTO THE ARENA...

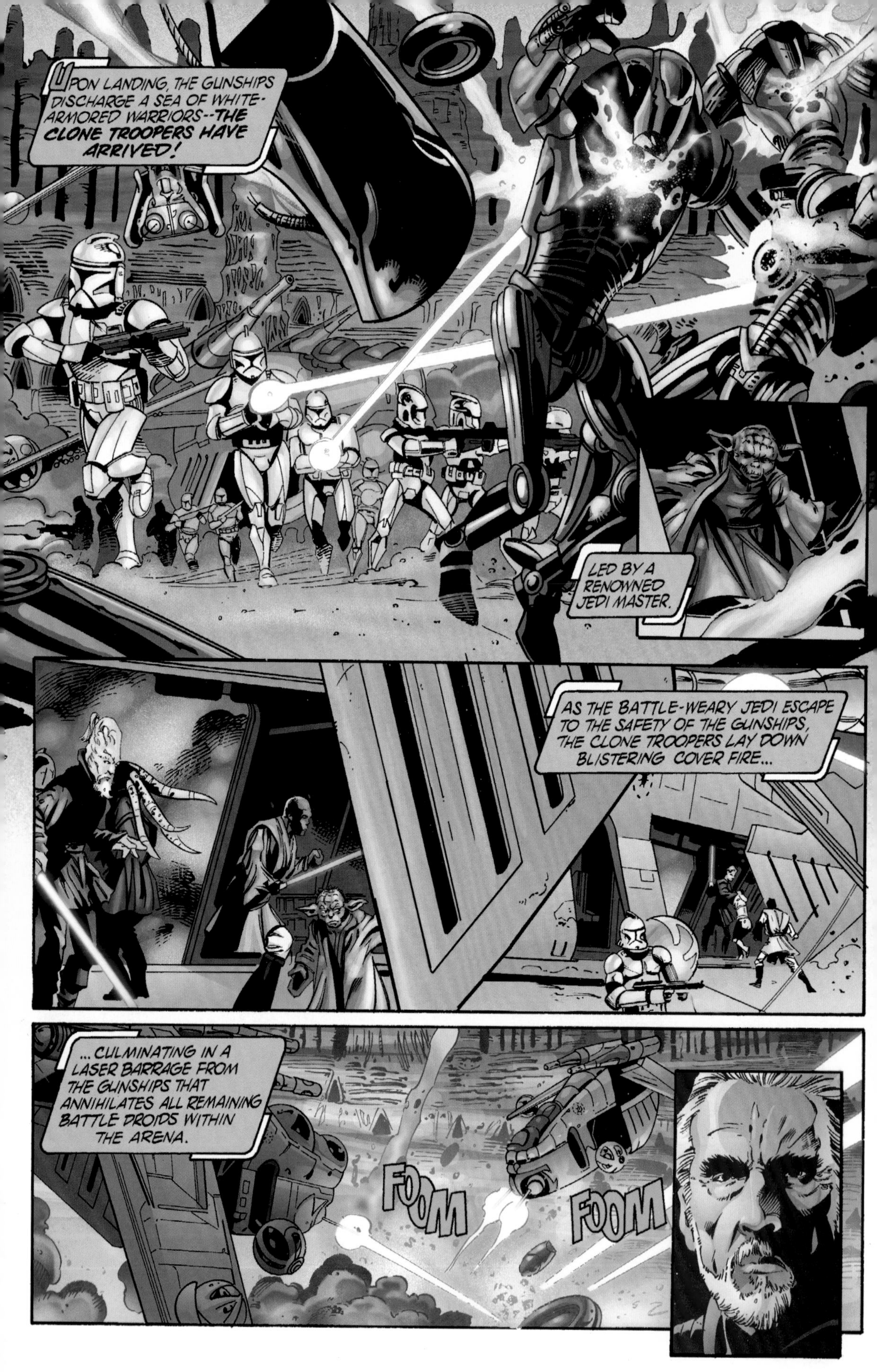
UPON LANDING, THE GUNSHIPS DISCHARGE A SEA OF WHITE-ARMORED WARRIORS--THE CLONE TROOPERS HAVE ARRIVED!
LED BY A RENOWNED JEDI MASTER.
AS THE BATTLE-WEARY JEDI ESCAPE TO THE SAFETY OF THE GUNSHIPS, THE CLONE TROOPERS LAY DOWN BLISTERING COVER FIRE...
...CULMINATING IN A LASER BARRAGE FROM THE GUNSHIPS THAT ANNIHILATES ALL REMAINING BATTLE DROIDS WITHIN THE ARENA.
FOOM
FOOM

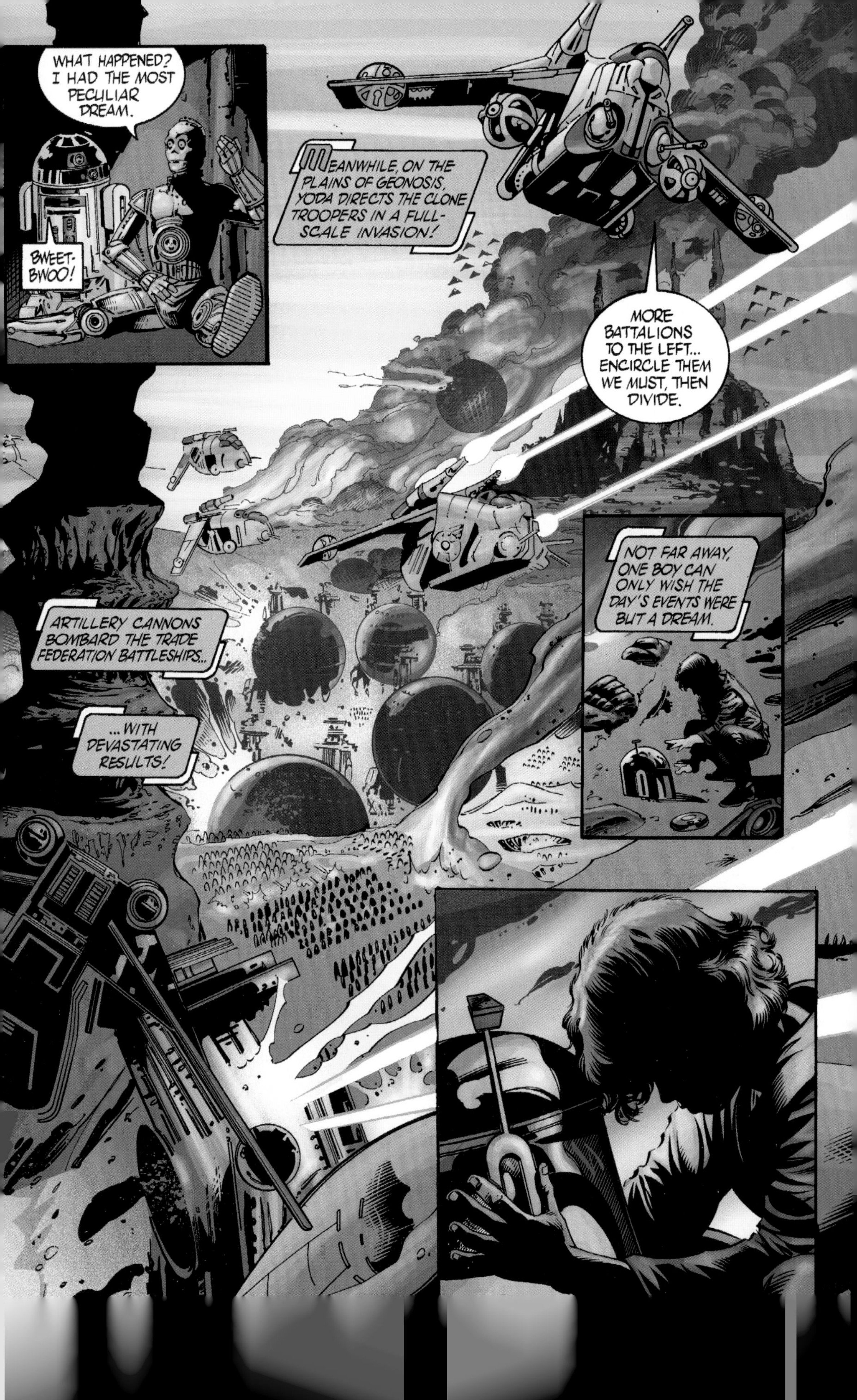
WHAT HAPPENED? I HAD THE MOST PECULIAR DREAM.
BWEET-BWOO!
MEANWHILE, ON THE PLAINS OF GEONOSIS, YODA DIRECTS THE CLONE TROOPERS IN A FULL-SCALE INVASION!
MORE BATTALIONS TO THE LEFT... ENCIRCLE THEM WE MUST, THEN DIVIDE.
ARTILLERY CANNONS BOMBARD THE TRADE FEDERATION BATTLESHIPS...
...WITH DEVASTATING RESULTS!
NOT FAR AWAY, ONE BOY CAN ONLY WISH THE DAY'S EVENTS WERE BUT A DREAM.

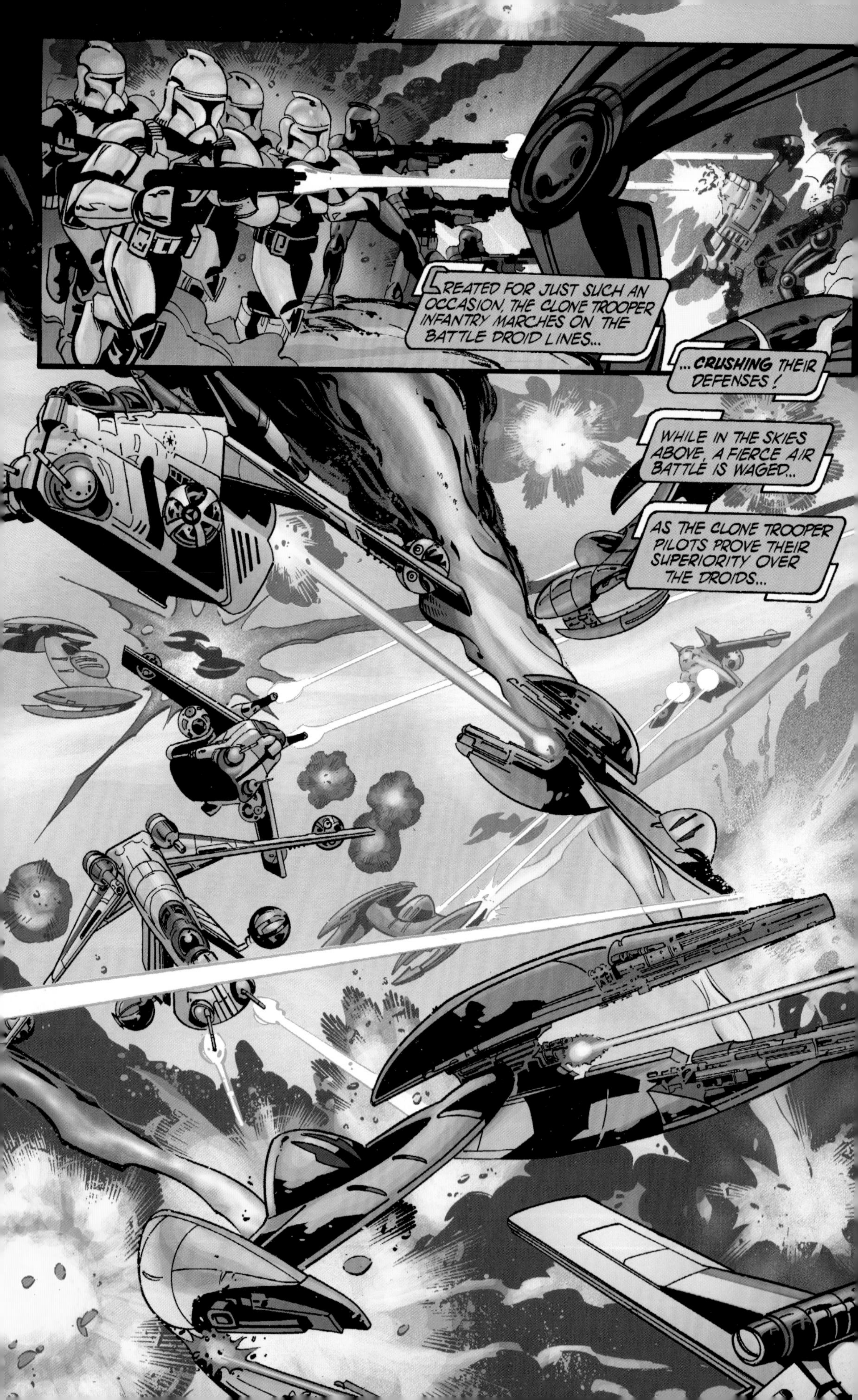
CREATED FOR JUST SUCH AN OCCASION, THE CLONE TROOPER INFANTRY MARCHES ON THE BATTLE DROID LINES...
...CRUSHING THEIR DEFENSES!
WHILE IN THE SKIES ABOVE, A FIERCE AIR BATTLE IS WAGED...
AS THE CLONE TROOPER PILOTS PROVE THEIR SUPERIORITY OVER THE DROIDS...

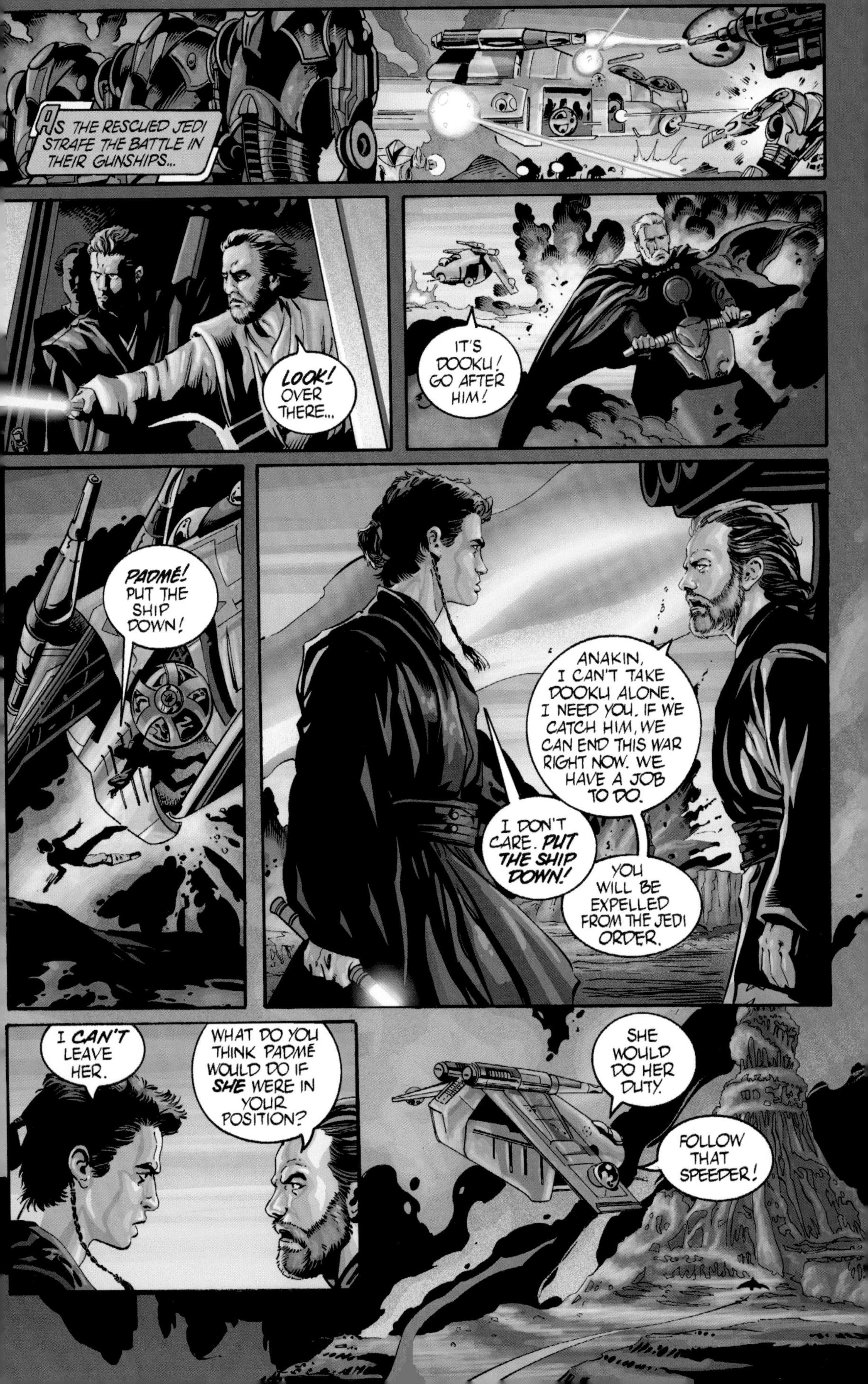
AS THE RESCUED JEDI STRAFE THE BATTLE IN THEIR GUNSHIPS...
LOOK! OVER THERE...
IT'S DOOKU! GO AFTER HIM!
PADMÉ! PUT THE SHIP DOWN!
ANAKIN, I CAN'T TAKE DOOKU ALONE. I NEED YOU. IF WE CATCH HIM, WE CAN END THIS WAR RIGHT NOW. WE HAVE A JOB TO DO.
I DON'T CARE. PUT THE SHIP DOWN!
YOU WILL BE EXPELLED FROM THE JEDI ORDER.
I CAN'T LEAVE HER.
WHAT DO YOU THINK PADMÉ WOULD DO IF SHE WERE IN YOUR POSITION?
SHE WOULD DO HER DUTY.
FOLLOW THAT SPEEDER!

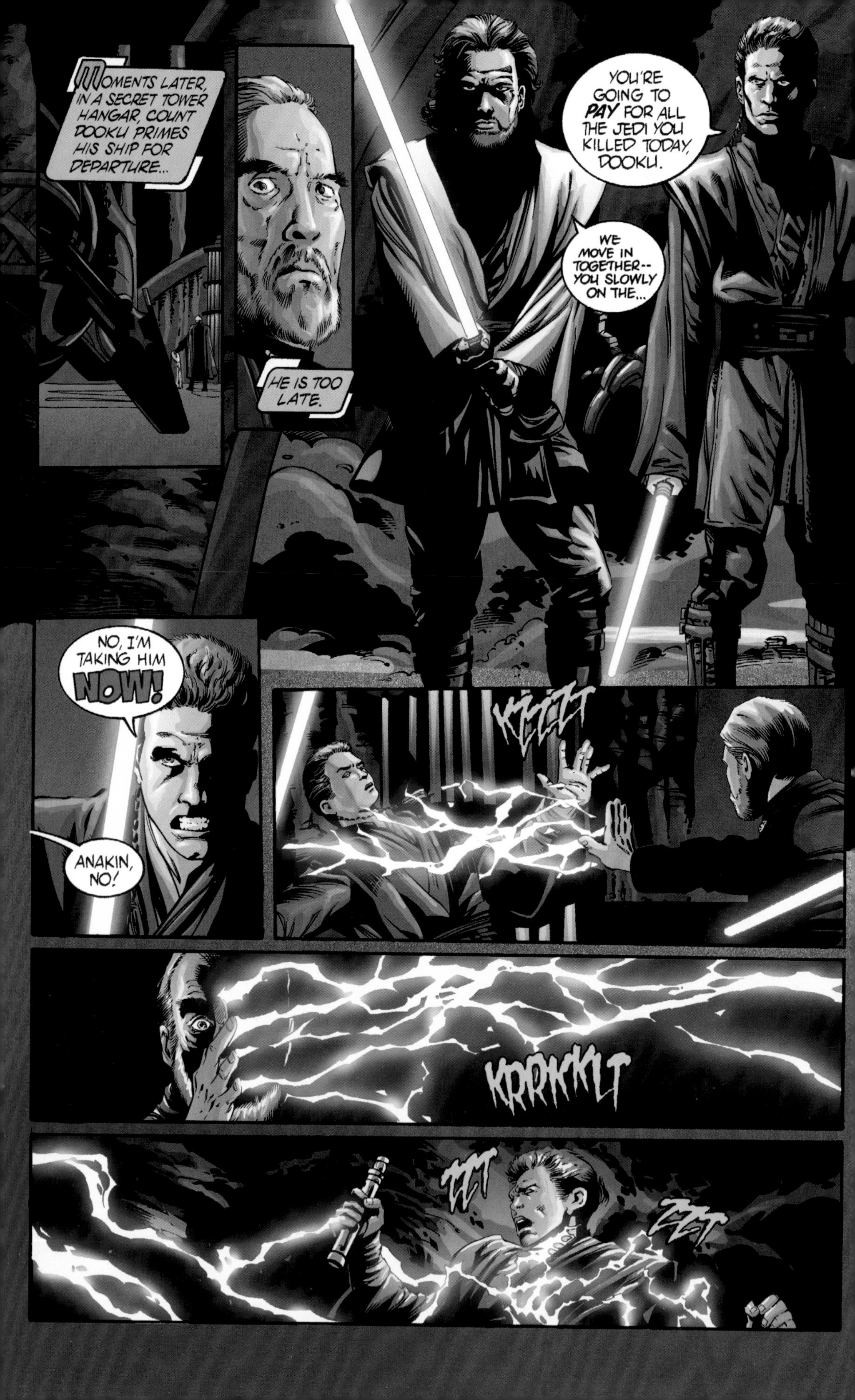
MOMENTS LATER, IN A SECRET TOWER HANGAR, COUNT DOOKU PRIMES HIS SHIP FOR DEPARTURE...
HE IS TOO LATE.
YOU'RE GOING TO PAY FOR ALL THE JEDI YOU KILLED TODAY, DOOKU.
WE MOVE IN TOGETHER-- YOU SLOWLY ON THE...
NO, I'M TAKING HIM NOW!
ANAKIN, NO!
KZZZT
KRRKKLT
ZZT
ZZZT

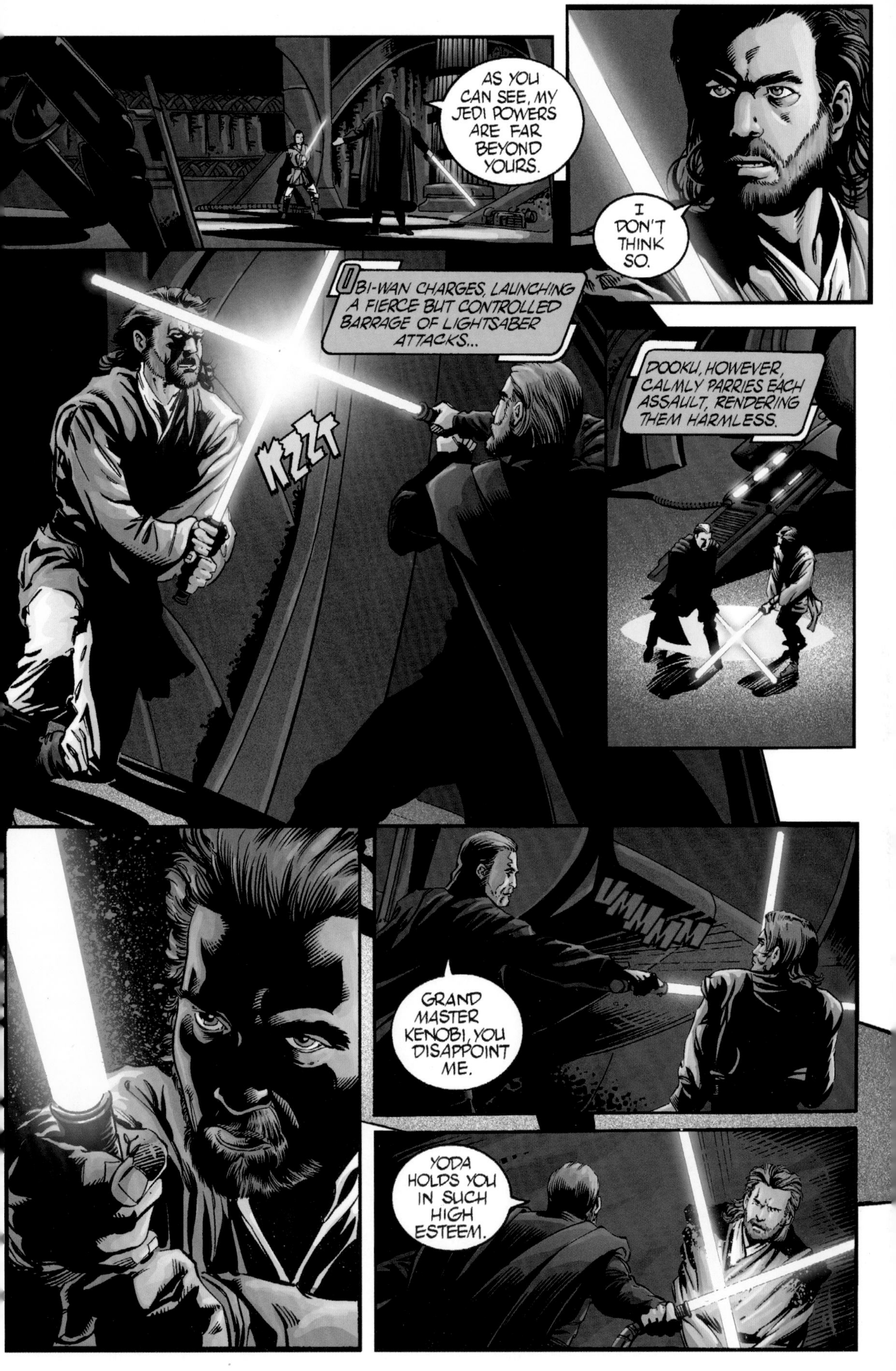
AS YOU CAN SEE, MY JEDI POWERS ARE FAR BEYOND YOURS.
I DON'T THINK SO.
OBI-WAN CHARGES, LAUNCHING A FIERCE BUT CONTROLLED BARRAGE OF LIGHTSABER ATTACKS...
KZZT
DOOKU, HOWEVER, CALMLY PARRIES EACH ASSAULT, RENDERING THEM HARMLESS.
UMMMM
GRAND MASTER KENOBI, YOU DISAPPOINT ME.
YODA HOLDS YOU IN SUCH HIGH ESTEEM.

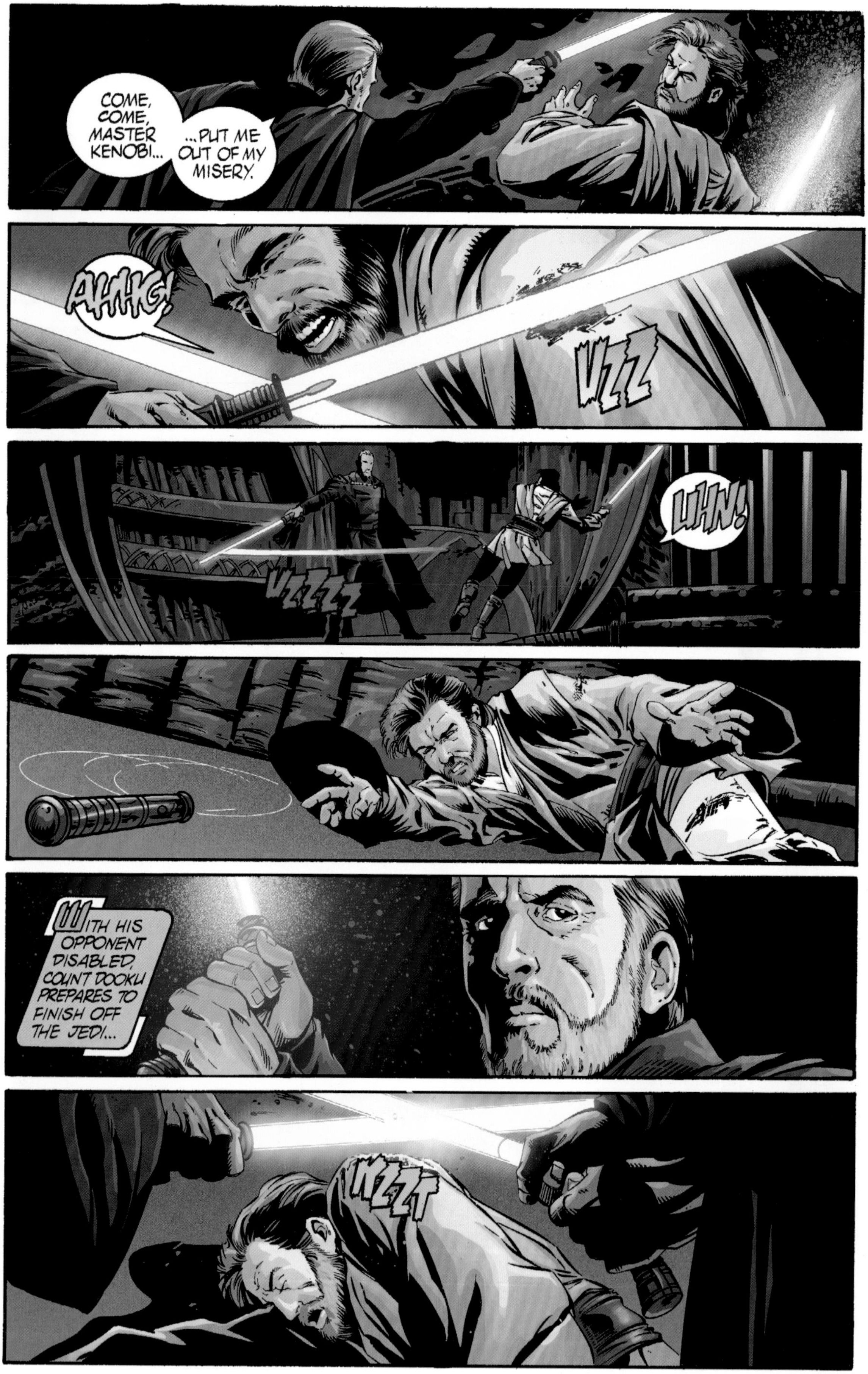
COME, COME, MASTER KENOBI...
...PUT ME OUT OF MY MISERY.
AHHG!
VZZ
UHN!
VZZZZ
WITH HIS OPPONENT DISABLED, COUNT DOOKU PREPARES TO FINISH OFF THE JEDI...
NZZT

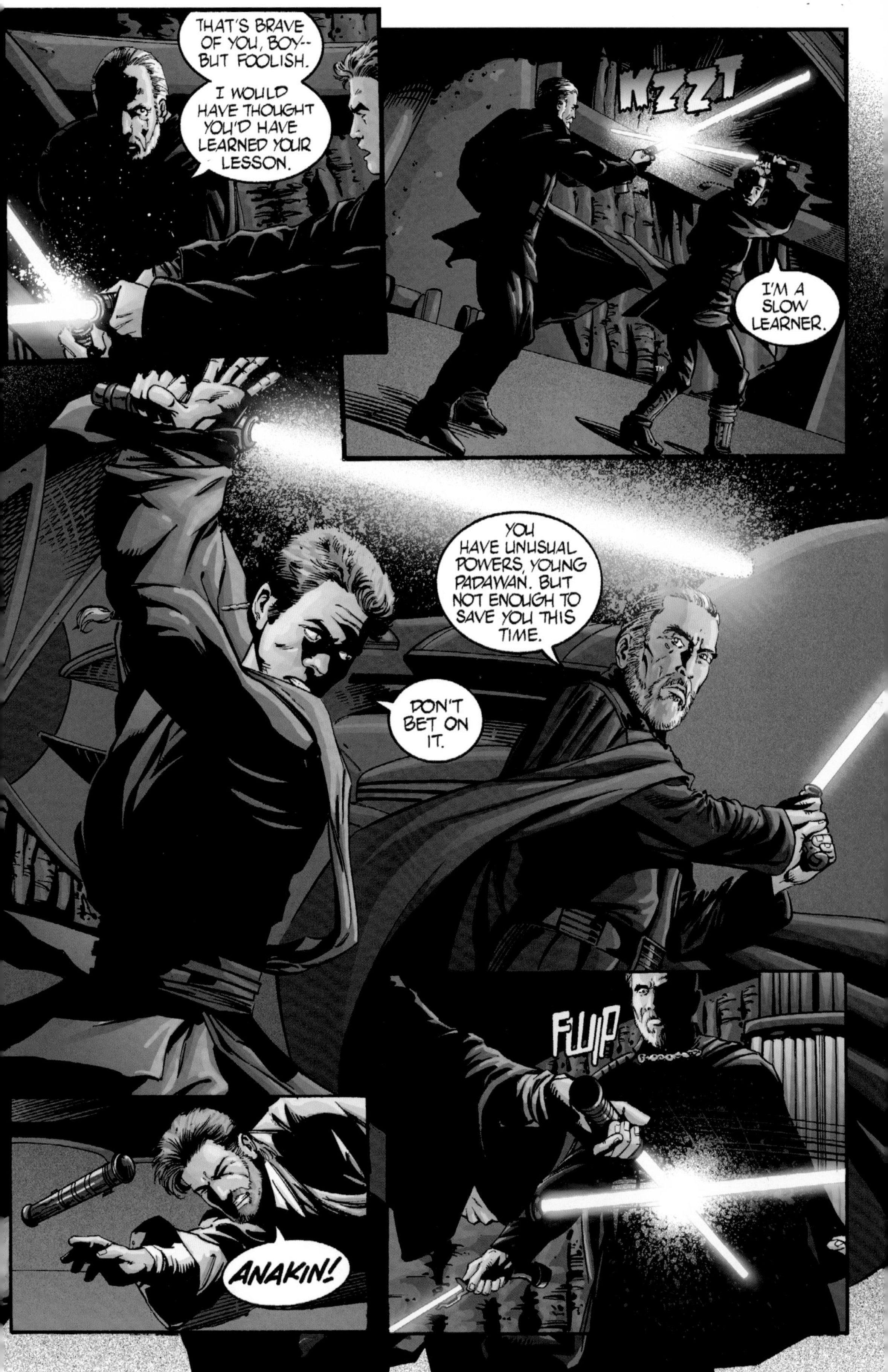
THAT'S BRAVE OF YOU, BOY-- BUT FOOLISH.
I WOULD HAVE THOUGHT YOU'D HAVE LEARNED YOUR LESSON.
NZZT
I'M A SLOW LEARNER.
YOU HAVE UNUSUAL POWERS, YOUNG PADAWAN. BUT NOT ENOUGH TO SAVE YOU THIS TIME.
DON'T BET ON IT.
FWIP
ANAKIN!

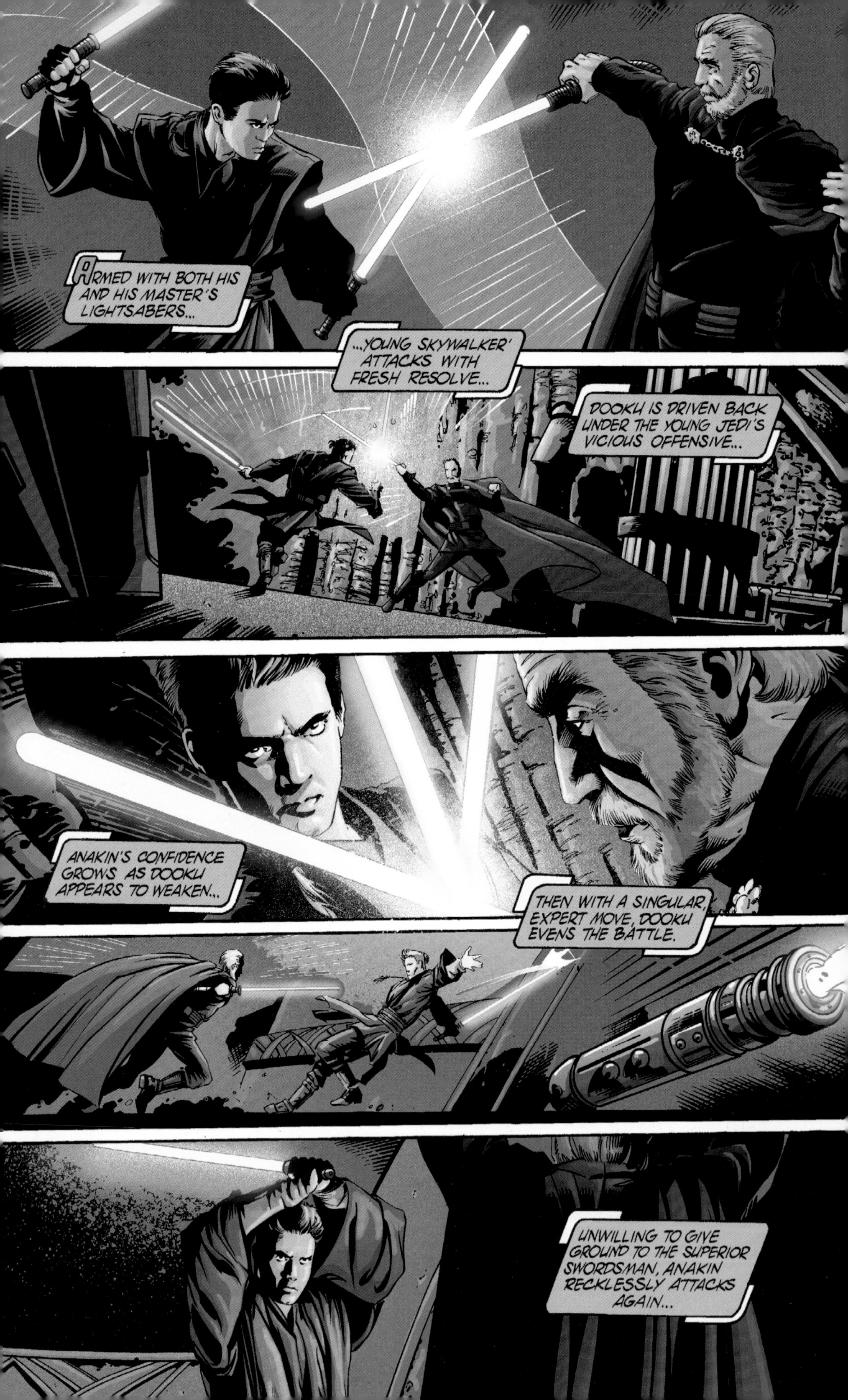
ARMED WITH BOTH HIS AND HIS MASTER'S LIGHTSABERS...
...YOUNG SKYWALKER' ATTACKS WITH FRESH RESOLVE...
DOOKU IS DRIVEN BACK UNDER THE YOUNG JEDI'S VICIOUS OFFENSIVE...
ANAKIN'S CONFIDENCE GROWS AS DOOKU APPEARS TO WEAKEN...
THEN WITH A SINGULAR, EXPERT MOVE, DOOKU EVENS THE BATTLE.
UNWILLING TO GIVE GROUND TO THE SUPERIOR SWORDSMAN, ANAKIN RECKLESSLY ATTACKS AGAIN...

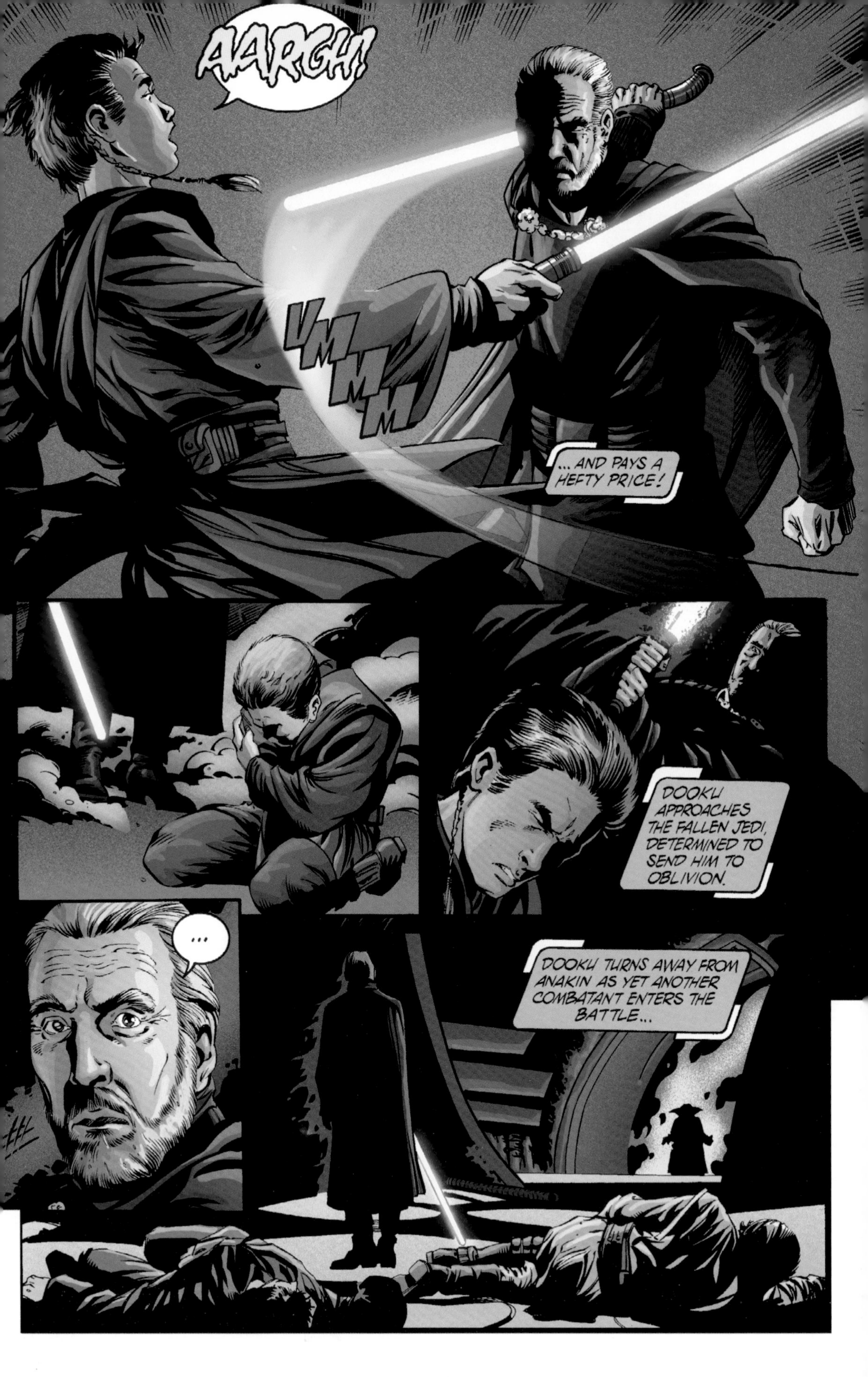
AARGH!
VMMMM
...AND PAYS A HEFTY PRICE!
DOOKU APPROACHES THE FALLEN JEDI, DETERMINED TO SEND HIM TO OBLIVION.
...
DOOKU TURNS AWAY FROM ANAKIN AS YET ANOTHER COMBATANT ENTERS THE BATTLE...

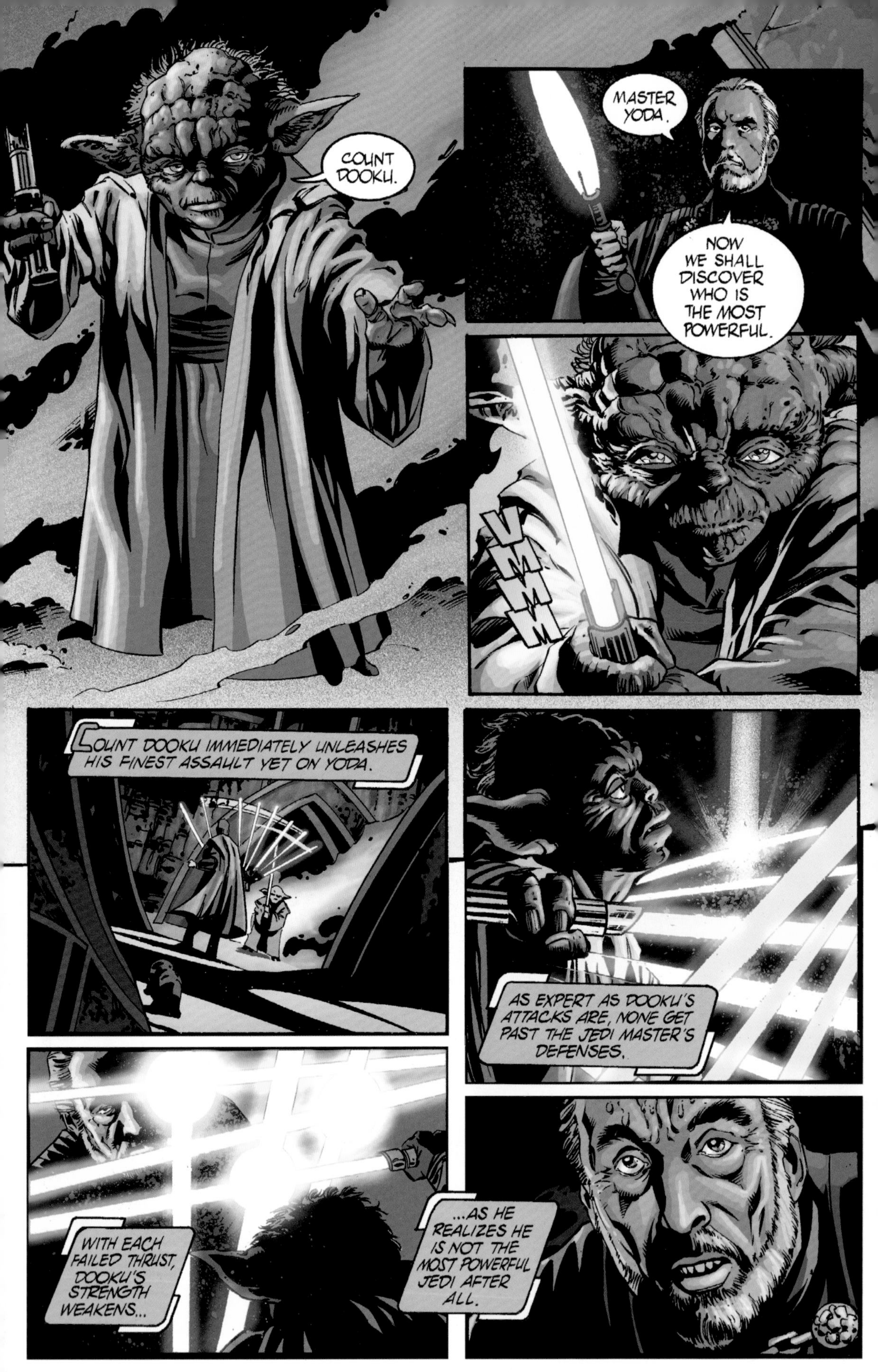
COUNT DOOKU.
MASTER YODA.
NOW WE SHALL DISCOVER WHO IS THE MOST POWERFUL.
VMMMM
COUNT DOOKU IMMEDIATELY UNLEASHES HIS FINEST ASSAULT YET ON YODA.
AS EXPERT AS DOOKU'S ATTACKS ARE, NONE GET PAST THE JEDI MASTER'S DEFENSES.
WITH EACH FAILED THRUST, DOOKU'S STRENGTH WEAKENS...
...AS HE REALIZES HE IS NOT THE MOST POWERFUL JEDI AFTER ALL.

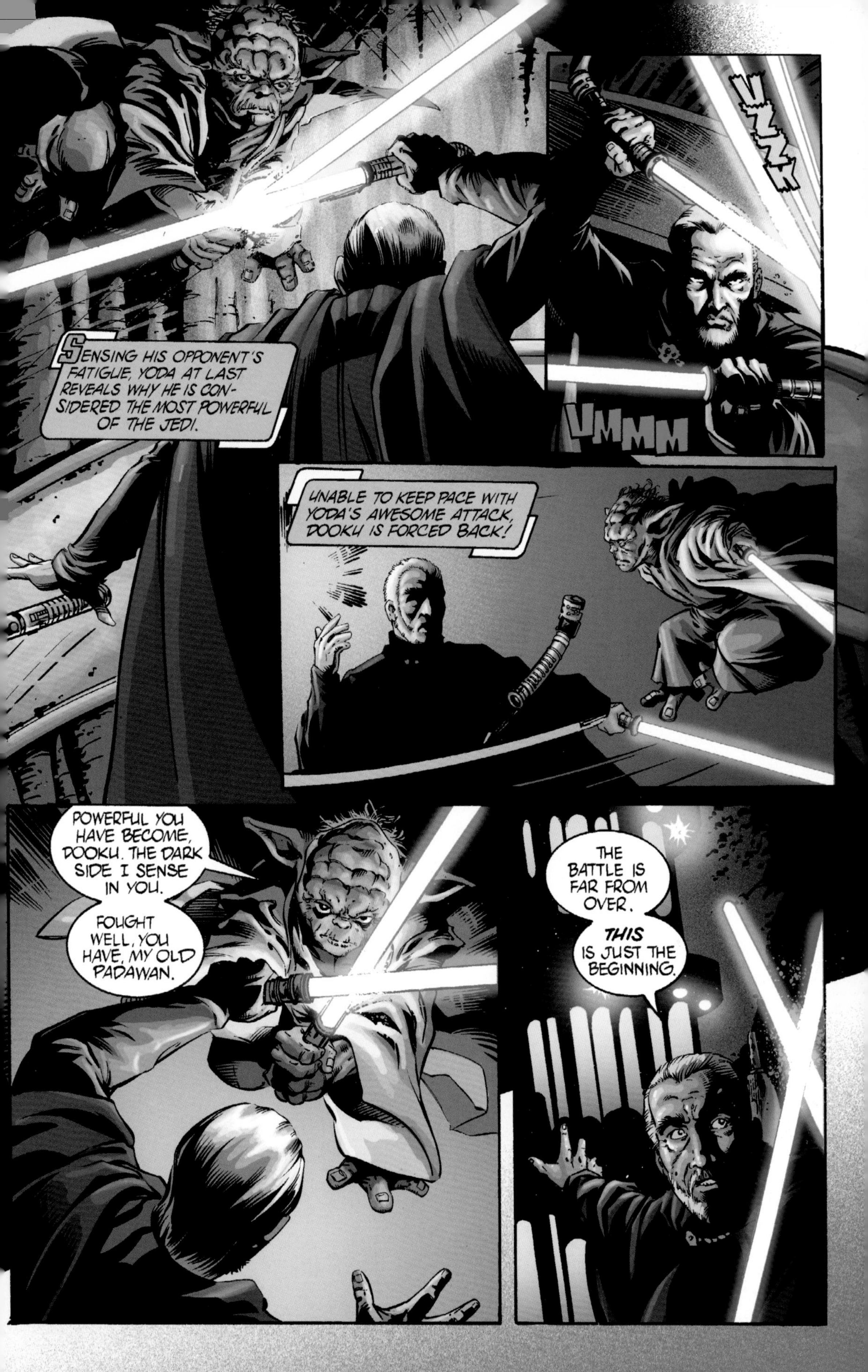
VZZZK
SENSING HIS OPPONENT'S FATIGUE, YODA AT LAST REVEALS WHY HE IS CONSIDERED THE MOST POWERFUL OF THE JEDI.
UMMM
UNABLE TO KEEP PACE WITH YODA'S AWESOME ATTACK, DOOKU IS FORCED BACK!
POWERFUL YOU HAVE BECOME, DOOKU. THE DARK SIDE I SENSE IN YOU.
FOUGHT WELL, YOU HAVE, MY OLD PADAWAN.
THE BATTLE IS FAR FROM OVER.
THIS IS JUST THE BEGINNING.

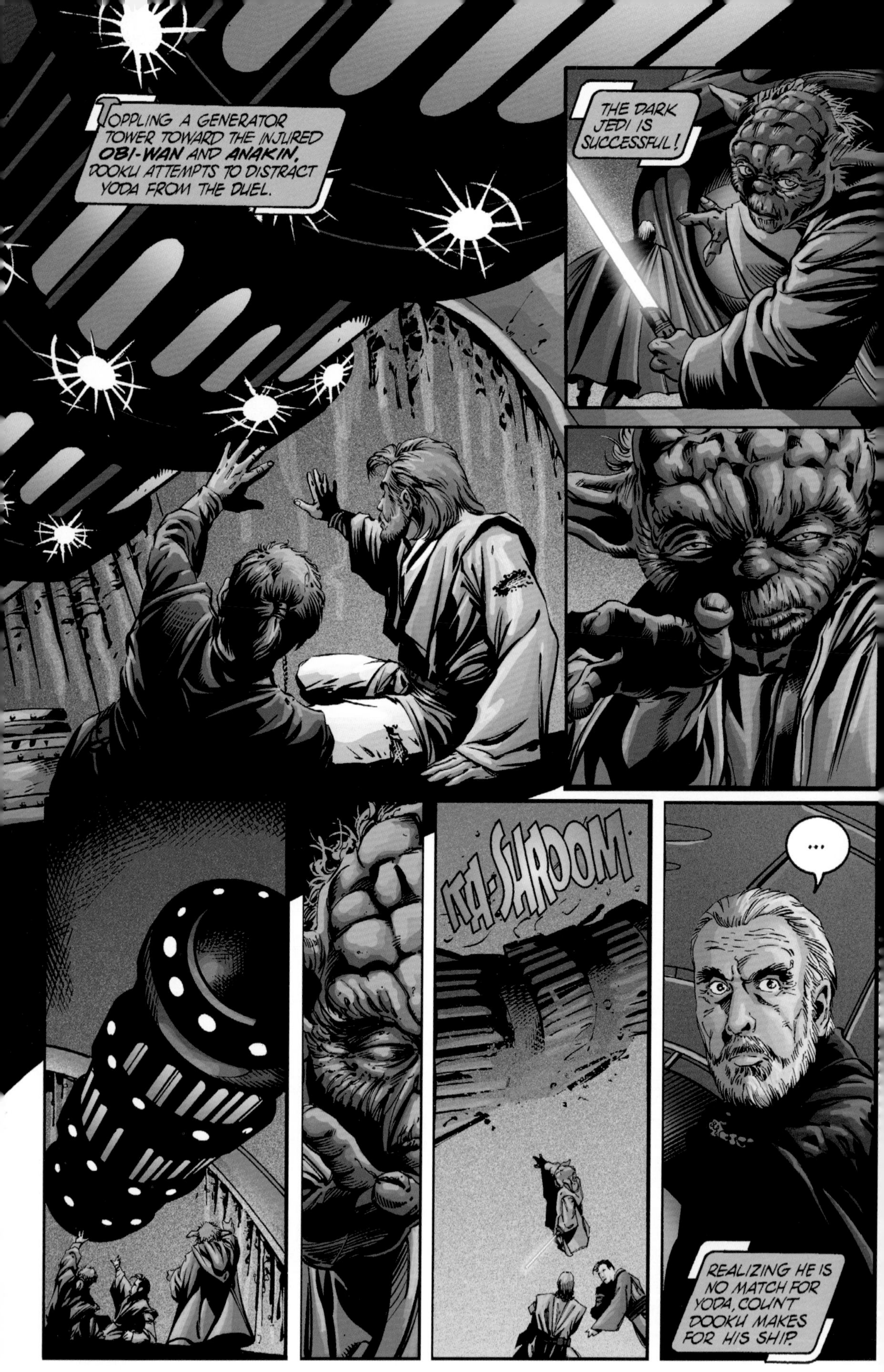
TOPPLING A GENERATOR TOWER TOWARD THE INJURED OBI-WAN AND ANAKIN, DOOKU ATTEMPTS TO DISTRACT YODA FROM THE DUEL.
THE DARK JEDI IS SUCCESSFUL!
KA-SHROOM
...
REALIZING HE IS NO MATCH FOR YODA, COUNT DOOKU MAKES FOR HIS SHIP.

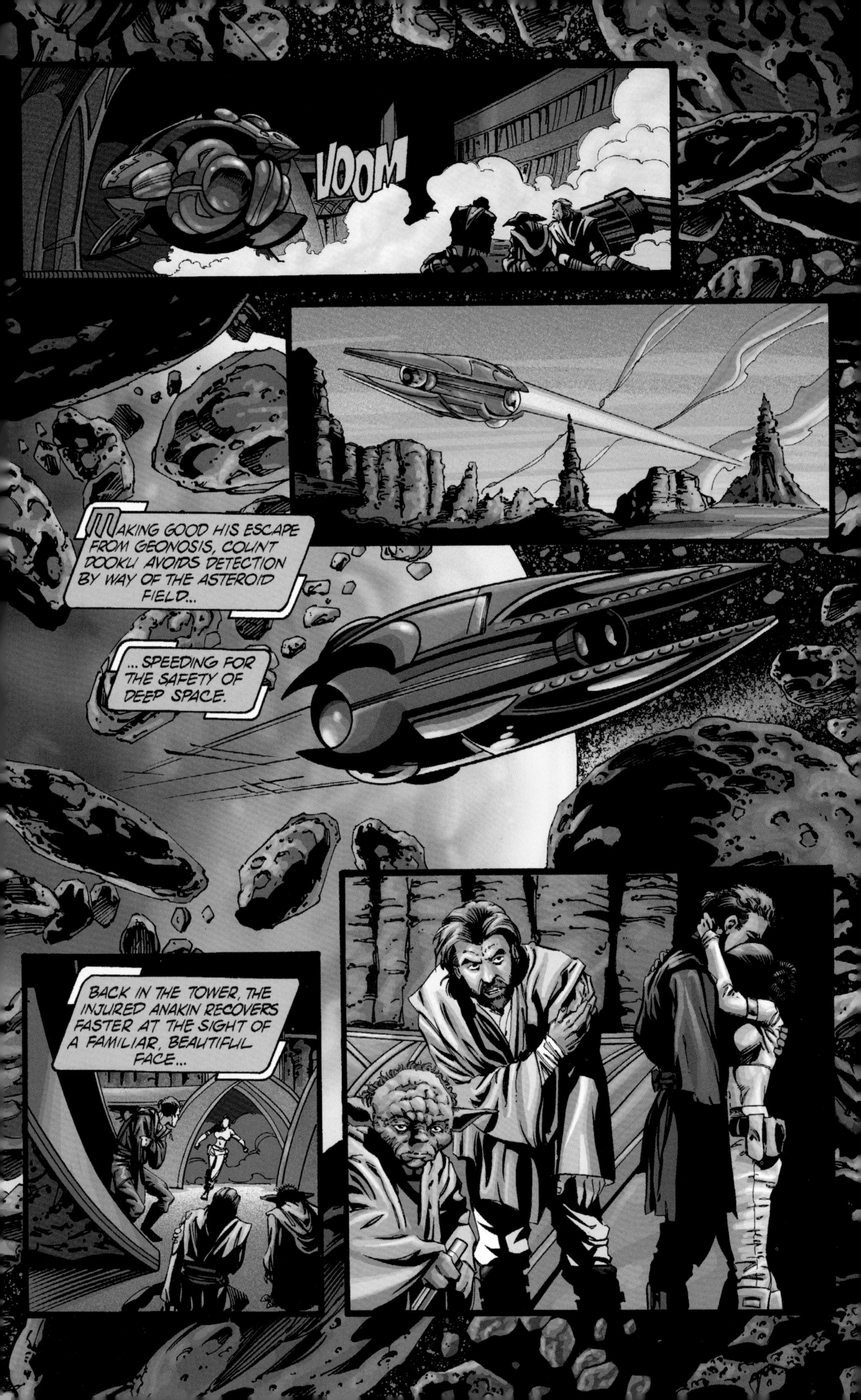
VOOM
MAKING GOOD HIS ESCAPE FROM GEONOSIS, COUNT DOOKU AVOIDS DETECTION BY WAY OF THE ASTEROID FIELD...
...SPEEDING FOR THE SAFETY OF DEEP SPACE.
BACK IN THE TOWER, THE INJURED ANAKIN RECOVERS FASTER AT THE SIGHT OF A FAMILIAR, BEAUTIFUL FACE...

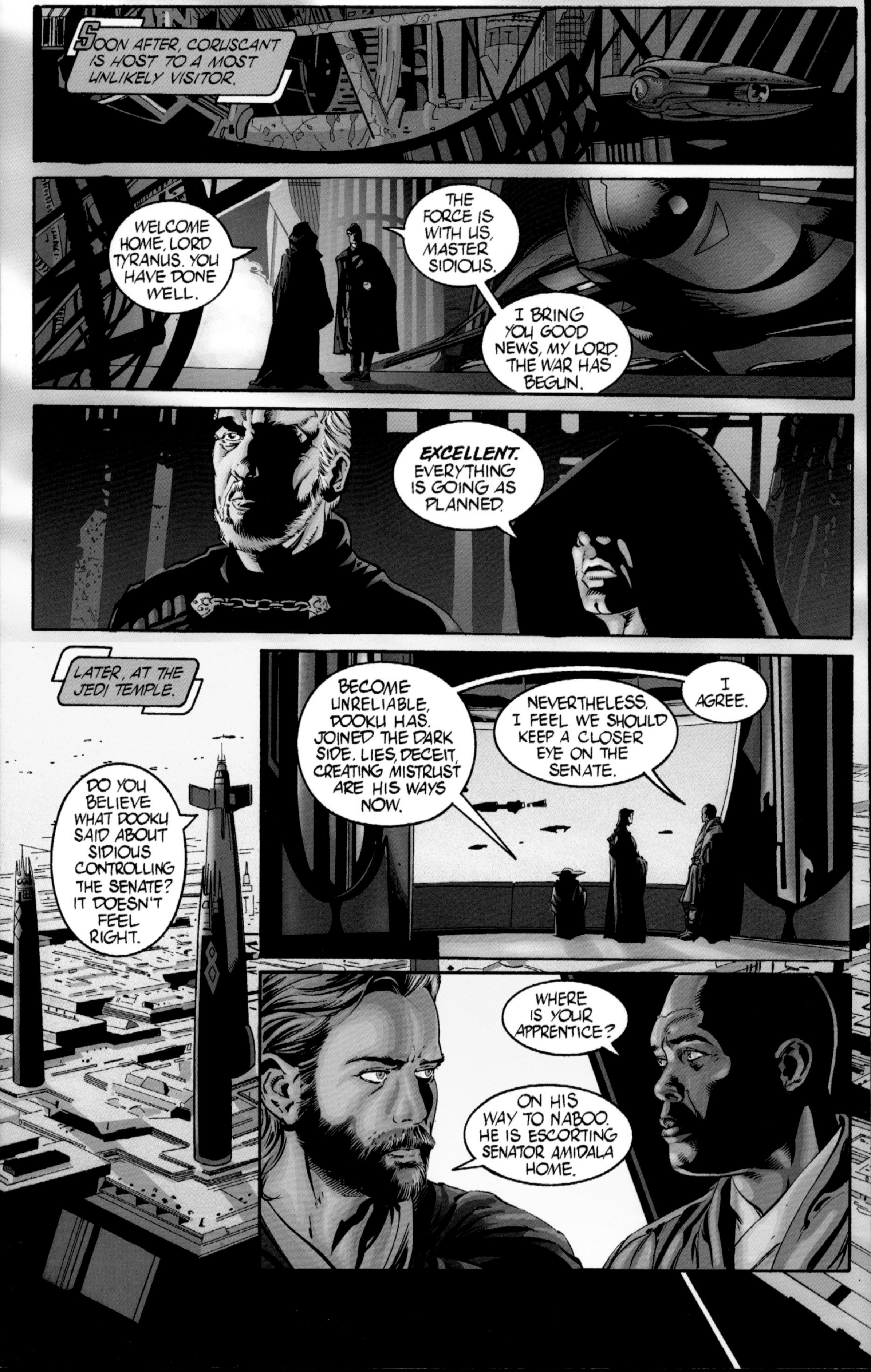

SOON AFTER, CORUSCANT IS HOST TO A MOST UNLIKELY VISITOR.
WELCOME HOME, LORD TYRANUS. YOU HAVE DONE WELL.
THE FORCE IS WITH US, MASTER SIDIOUS.
I BRING YOU GOOD NEWS, MY LORD. THE WAR HAS BEGUN.
EXCELLENT. EVERYTHING IS GOING AS PLANNED.
LATER, AT THE JEDI TEMPLE.
DO YOU BELIEVE WHAT DOOKU SAID ABOUT SIDIOUS CONTROLLING THE SENATE? IT DOESN'T FEEL RIGHT.
BECOME UNRELIABLE, DOOKU HAS. JOINED THE DARK SIDE. LIES, DECEIT, CREATING MISTRUST ARE HIS WAYS NOW.
I AGREE.
NEVERTHELESS, I FEEL WE SHOULD KEEP A CLOSER EYE ON THE SENATE.
WHERE IS YOUR APPRENTICE?
ON HIS WAY TO NABOO. HE IS ESCORTING SENATOR AMIDALA HOME.

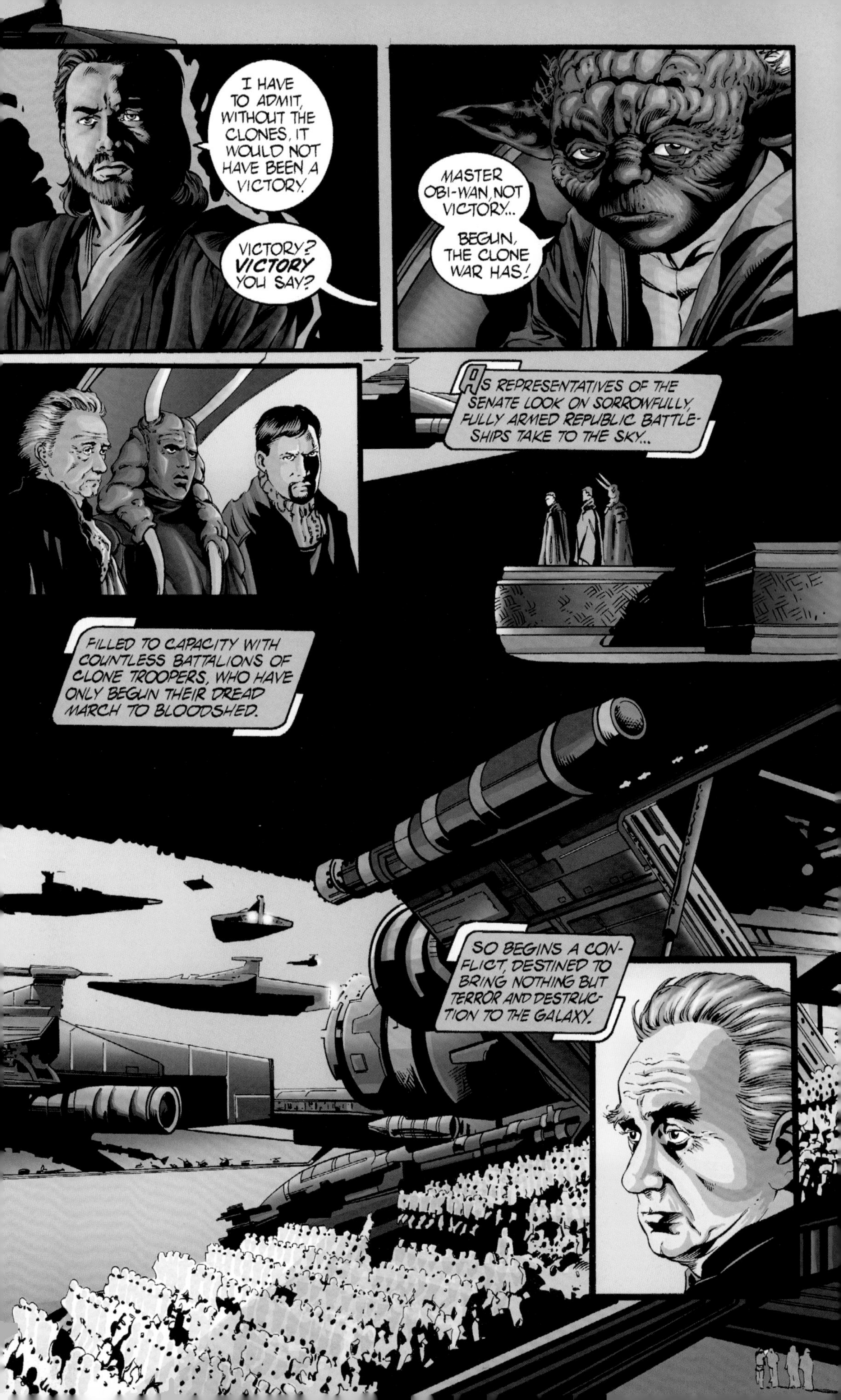

I HAVE TO ADMIT, WITHOUT THE CLONES, IT WOULD NOT HAVE BEEN A VICTORY.
VICTORY? VICTORY YOU SAY?
MASTER OBI-WAN, NOT VICTORY...
BEGUN, THE CLONE WAR HAS!
AS REPRESENTATIVES OF THE SENATE LOOK ON SORROWFULLY, FULLY ARMED REPUBLIC BATTLE-SHIPS TAKE TO THE SKY...
FILLED TO CAPACITY WITH COUNTLESS BATTALIONS OF CLONE TROOPERS, WHO HAVE ONLY BEGUN THEIR DREAD MARCH TO BLOODSHED.
SO BEGINS A CON-FLICT, DESTINED TO BRING NOTHING BUT TERROR AND DESTRUC-TION TO THE GALAXY.

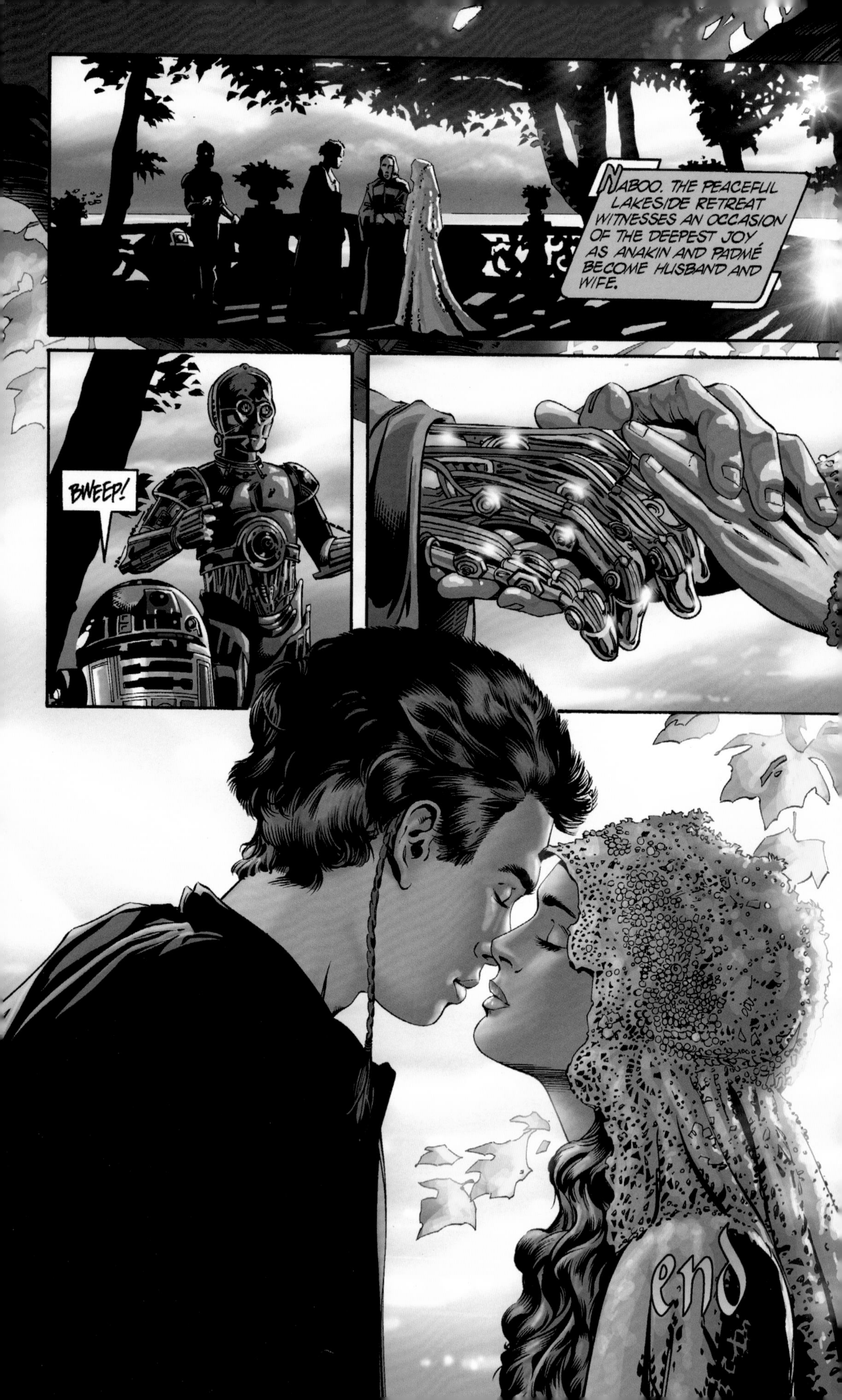
NABOO. THE PEACEFUL LAKESIDE RETREAT WITNESSES AN OCCASION OF THE DEEPEST JOY AS ANAKIN AND PADMÉ BECOME HUSBAND AND WIFE.
BWEEP!
end

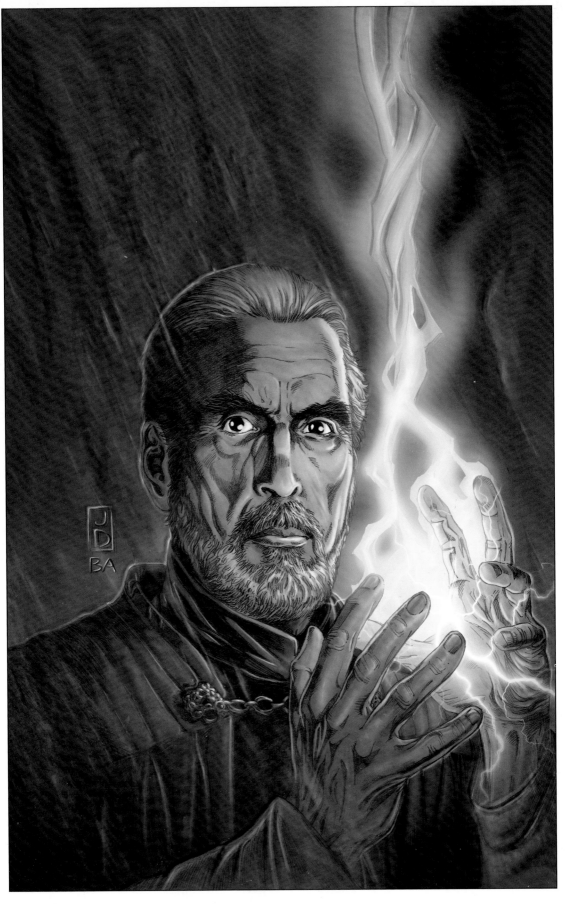

PENCILS BY **JAN DUURSEMA**
COLORS BY **BRAD ANDERSON**

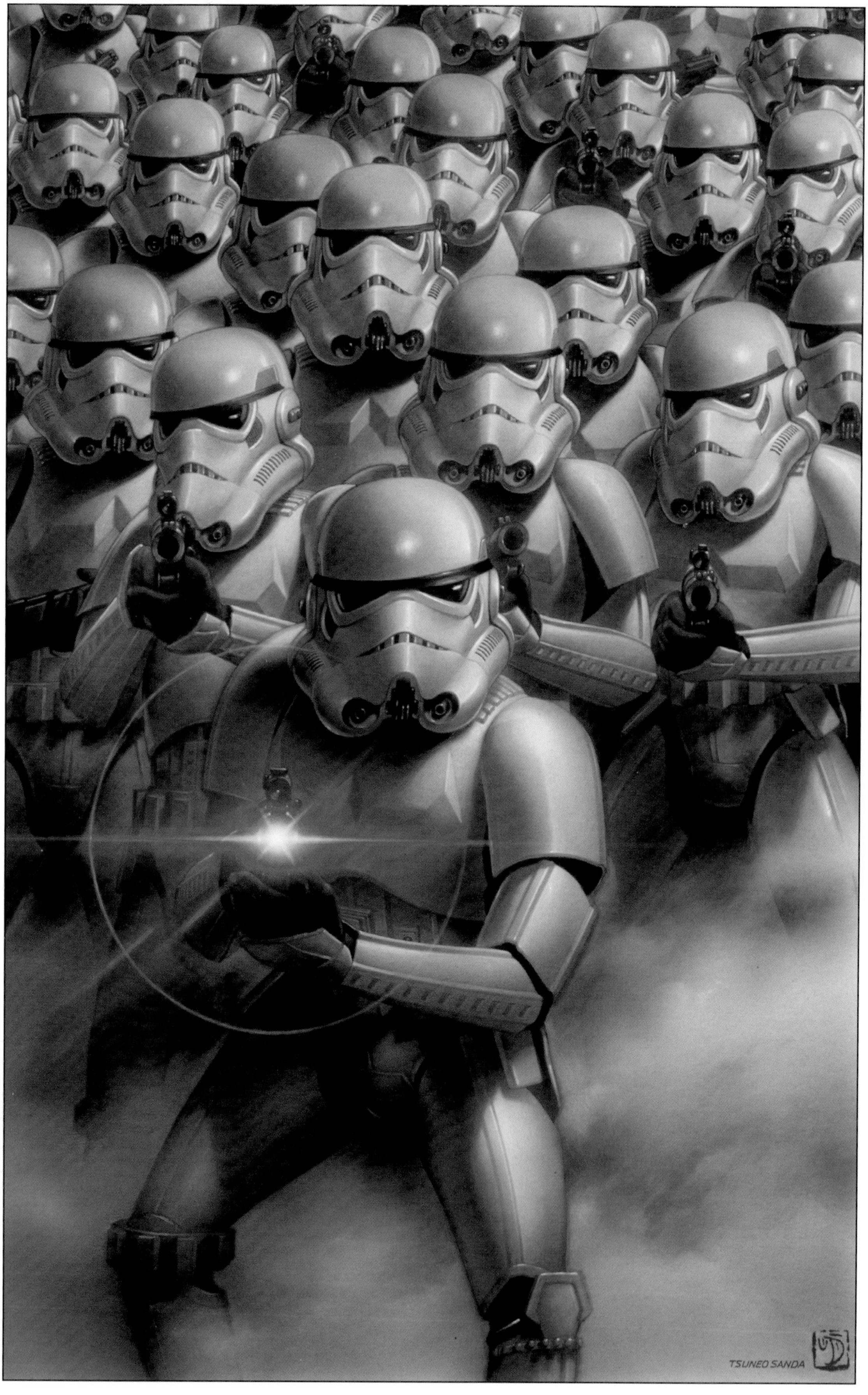
TSUNEO SANDA

ART BY **TSUNEO SANDA**